THE MALONEYS' MAGICAL WEATHERBOX

THE MALONEYS' MAGICAL WEATHERBOX

NIGEL QUINLAN

Louisburg Library
Bringing People and Information Together

ROARING BROOK PRESS
NEW YORK

Copyright © 2015 by Nigel Quinlan
Published by Roaring Brook Press
Roaring Brook Press is a division of Holtzbrinck Publishing Holdings Limited Partnership
175 Fifth Avenue, New York, New York 10010
mackids.com

Library of Congress Cataloging-in-Publication Data

Quinlan, Nigel.
    The Maloneys' magical weatherbox / Nigel Quinlan. — First edition.
        pages cm
    Summary: When autumn fails to arrive at the end of summer, Irish siblings
Neil and Liz must battle for control of the seasons from the evil Mrs. Fitzgerald.
    ISBN 978-1-62672-033-6 (hardback) — ISBN 978-1-62672-034-3 (e-book)
    [1. Seasons—Fiction. 2. Weather—Fiction. 3. Magic—Fiction. 4. Brothers and
sisters—Fiction.] I. Title.
    PZ7.1.Q53Mal 2015
    [Fic]—dc23

                                                            2014043117

Roaring Brook Press books may be purchased for business or promotional use. For
information on bulk purchases please contact Macmillan Corporate and Premium Sales
Department at (800) 221-7945 x5442 or by email at specialmarkets@macmillan.com.

First edition 2015
Printed in the United States of America by R. R. Donnelley & Sons Company,
Harrisonburg, Virginia

1 3 5 7 9 10 8 6 4 2

*To my dear friend Kasey, as well as her
Mom and Pop, Joan and Dave, and all their
friends and neighbors and relatives who are
as kind and hospitable a bunch o' folk as you
could hope to meet anywhere, let alone the
wilds of Connecticut.*

PART 1

The Maloneys' Legendary B&B

CHAPTER 1

NEIL

There's Mum and Dad and me and Liz, my younger sister—who's mad and dangerous so watch out—and our little brother, Owen, who's as soft as wet soap and needs looking out for. We're the Maloneys, and once upon a time we lived together in a house in the middle of Ireland— the bit they call the Midlands in case anyone gets confused about which part of the country they're living in and to remind them that they're not actually in any danger of falling into the sea. The house was called Maloneys' Bed and Breakfast, and there were always people staying with us, and Mum was always using us like slaves and servants, cruelly making us do jobs like cleaning up and sweeping the floor and changing the sheets and filling the dishwasher.

Summer was the busiest. We'd get tourists driving or biking or hiking around the country. A lot of them didn't speak English. Mostly they were nice, friendly people, and sometimes they had kids who would stay a few days and we'd make friends for a while. Then they'd go away and we'd never see them again, which was kind of sad. Sometimes we promised to write, but we never did.

"Back to being the Lonely Maloneys," Liz would say, and run off into the woods or climb up onto the roof or do a strange dance in the middle of the lawn.

Mum was in charge of the bed and breakfast, doing the booking and the cooking and some of the cleaning, except for most of it, which her slaves had to do for her.

Our dad was the Weatherman. Our dad was one of the Most Important People in the World.

That was one of our secrets.

Here's another . . .

Outside the B&B there was an old-fashioned wooden phone box, the sort nobody uses anymore. We called it the Weatherbox. The phone inside rang only four times a year and only my dad answered it. When he did, something amazing happened: the Season changed. The old Season left, and the new Season came through the phone and went to work making things warmer or colder or wetter or drier or whatever it wanted to do.

There are only four special places with four special people like this in all the world. There's the hollow of an ancient tree. There's a deep underground chamber.

There's the summit of a holy mountain. And there was our Weatherbox.

When Summer arrived that year, the last year Summer arrived, everything seemed fine. Everything seemed normal. We walked, all together in the early morning, down from the house to the gate, rubbing sleep from our eyes. Owen held mum's hand tight, and Liz was doing her weird dancing and her weird chanting. She used to get me to do the dancing and the chanting with her, but I don't do that anymore.

The sky got brighter. The stars and the planets all faded away, and there was a tiny sliver of moon lying on its back like God's coat hook. Mum put the thick blanket down on the wall. We sat on it and draped it over our shoulders to keep out the chill, and we waited, and we watched the Weatherbox grow solid and real as the morning light spread around us. Molten gold began to flow into the sky behind the house. The few cottony clouds were glowing. An airplane laid a snail's trail of white vapor across the rim of the sky, and the twin white lines were like a welcome mat laid out for the sun.

We waited, and we watched, and when the tip of the sun rose above the horizon and the light touched the words carved above the door of the Weatherbox, the phone began to ring.

Dad, the Weatherman, opened the door. It swung easily, heavily on its hinges, while large springs at the top and bottom tried to pull it closed again. Dad stepped inside and

5

let the door shut, and we heard the ringing stop as he picked up the phone and put it to his ear. It was hard to see through the small square panes of glass into the darkness of the box, but Dad seemed to change. For a moment he became something else.

I don't remember ever really seeing what happened, not clearly. What I remember is the smell. Summer came pouring from the box, and it was . . .

the sweetness of flowers . . .

and fruits . . .

and warm sand . . .

and deep waters . . .

and cut grass . . .

and insects buzzing . . .

and birdsong . . .

and endless days . . .

and hot sun . . .

and cool showers.

I laughed and danced and sang, and Mum and Liz and Owen laughed and danced and sang with me. It was the most perfect, beautiful magic.

Then we went in for breakfast. We had pancakes, as usual, and after that we had a Summer. We didn't know it was going to be the last one before everything went wrong. We didn't even begin to know until the Tourist arrived, the day before the Autumn.

CHAPTER 2

LIZ

It was me that met the Tourist first. It was me that saw the hags first, too, and the bog beast, though Owen was with me at the time.

The Day of the Tourist, which was when it all started, was bright and warm and sunny—September twenty-first. I decided I was a hawk and climbed up the wall and up the tree and up the drainpipe until I was perched on the roof beside the chimney. There was no breeze. No birds flying or singing. Sometimes a car went past. Sometimes I ruffled my feathers and flapped my wings, ready to spring into the air and fly.

It had been a Summer of extremely Weird Weather, so I had decided to be particularly alert coming up to the day the new Season was to arrive. Dad told us that there'd been Weird Weather every couple of years since he and

Granddad moved from the farm, but this Summer had been pure hectic. Not a week had gone by without Weird Weather breaking out all over us. In June we had hailstones the size of golf balls. Umbrellas were useless so Dad made us wooden shields that we held over our heads while we pelted like rabbits to and from the house. In July we had multicolored rain—starting with black, then red, then green, then yellow, and then flippin' purple! It was from all different types of dust and sand and mud and muck being swept up by winds, mixed in with the moisture, carried through the atmosphere, and then falling in the raindrops all over our house and garden. Purple precipitation, Dad called it.

Dad was usually able to cut the Weird Weather short fairly sharpish, no bother, except he always found fogs tricky, which was why we spent three weeks in August under a white block of fog. It was like being blind, and everything sounded funny, but the fog itself stretched only about fifty yards in each direction.

"So what the heck's going on, Dad?' we asked him.

And Dad furrowed his brow and chewed his lip and didn't answer.

Anyway, there was no sign of any Weird Weather trying to sneak up on us that afternoon, so I decided to stop being a hawk, climb down off the roof, and go patrol the woods.

Long ago, I'd made up my mind that I was going to be a Shieldsman when I grew up. It's the Shieldsmen's job to protect the Weatherman. Way back in the days when the Doorway was protected by a fort that stood beside where Loch Farny is now, that was where the Weatherman, the Shieldsmen, and the Weathermages all lived together for hundreds of years until the Weatherman threw them out, knocked down the fort, and built a farm because things like guns and cannons had made forts next to useless.

"Go hide," the Weatherman told the Shieldsmen and the Weathermages. "Do your duty, but be quiet about it."

And they did. Some people may have decided the farm would make a nice prize and tried to attack, but they never reached it. Bandits, rebels, redcoats: none of them so much as set foot on the hill. They all went into the bogs and the woods and the glens, and they never came out.

After a few hundred years, however, the Weathermages got tired of hiding in ditches, wandering the roads, fighting nasty, sneaky battles, and chasing the rich and powerful to recruit them or warn them off. They left the Shieldsmen to do the dirty work and decided they preferred to protect the Weatherman from the luxury and comfort of somewhere warm and dry, where the rich and powerful could come to them, and rebels, bandits, and redcoats were unpleasant rumors that occasionally disrupted the traffic and startled the servants. They opened an extremely exclusive and snooty gentlemen's club in Dublin, the Weathermen's Club. Its members were rich and powerful secret Weathermages, and they had rich and powerful friends in politics and business and the military. Everything the club did was designed to hide what went on in one small farm in the Midlands.

And so the Doorway—where each Season comes through—was well protected from everything. Well, nearly everything.

Dad was the Weatherman now, and Neil was going to be Weatherman one day. I couldn't be the Weatherman because I hadn't been born first. If I had been born first I still couldn't be the Weatherman because I'm a girl. They told me there had never been a girl Weatherman. I told them I thought they were wrong and that hundreds and hundreds of years ago someone decided they didn't like girls being in charge of anything, so they made up a rule saying only boys could be Weathermen and pretended that it had always been that way. Dad said this was a conspiracy theory, but I pointed out how much effort boys put into making sure girls aren't in charge, or, if they are in charge, pretending they weren't all through history. Dad just said, "Hmmm."

So, I was going to be a Shieldsman. But the Shieldsmen were all gone so I was learning how all by myself.

I went into the house and got my bow and my arrows and went down the path and through the front gate, testing the string on my bow and making sure the feathers in my hair weren't going to fall out. It's moments like that,

when you're distracted by small things, that the unex-
pected sneaks up on you . . .

"That's a very nice bow," someone said.

I jumped and dropped the bow, both of which are unfor-
giveable for a Shieldsman. The man was big and wide, wearing faded jeans and a big checked shirt, which were full of
his fat and his muscle, and he had a huge dark beard that
exploded from his face in all directions like a clump of wild
moss. As I looked up at him, he seemed to fill the sky, while
under the beard was an apologetic smile and eager eyes.

I couldn't understand how someone so big could have
snuck up on me like that.

"Sorry," he said, and he dropped the suitcase he was
carrying and bent down to pick up my bow, and then dropped
the other suitcase he was pulling behind him on little wheels.
He turned to catch it, still bent over, and his fingers got tangled in the handle and he tripped over the other suitcase and
fell sort of sideways, like a mountain tilting over, but he was
so big and wide he didn't fall fully; instead he went down on
one knee, waving his arms for balance, and the suitcase on
wheels went flying out of his hand and over the wall. The
lid popped open and clothes spilled everywhere. He lurched
after it, kicking the other suitcase, which also sprang
open, and books and books and more books, flapping like
crows—a murder of books—went flying all over the road.

I grabbed my bow and ran for the woods.

CHAPTER 3

NEIL

It was as if, I don't know, a giant balloon made out of extra-extra-large clown costumes stitched together had exploded all over the front lawn. Enormous checked shirts and stiff denim jeans and woolen socks and long underwear lay everywhere. If we'd hoisted one of the shirts like a sail over one of the pairs of jeans, the whole family could have gone floating down the Shannon. We could have built a small cottage out of all the books, which had spilled out onto the road as if a library had sprung a leak.

"Sorry!" said the Tourist as he tried to stuff everything back into his suitcase. "I had a . . . I saw a . . . There was a girl with a bow and then, well, I—er—Sorry."

"And where did Liz go?" Mum asked as she and Dad folded the ends of a tent-sized sweater together.

"Oh, across the road into the woods. I think I scared her."

"Scared?" I said. "Liz?"

"My name's Ed," said the Tourist. "Ed Wharton. Uh, I booked a room . . ."

"Yes, Mr. Wharton, that's right," Mum said. We had the clothes and the books more or less repacked. Dad carried one suitcase, and I pulled the other along while Owen pushed. Mum held the door open and invited Ed Wharton inside.

"Great!" said Ed, striding up the path. "I've been driving for half the day. It's great to finally be here. I drive a truck for a living—left it parked up the road there a bit; I hope nobody minds. Didn't think you'd want a great big truck blocking your drive. Lovely house. What a view! And that phone box—classic design! And so well maintained! You do that yourself, do you? So nice to see people looking after their heritage. Well done, well done!"

I think I was the only one who noticed Owen's head go up at the mention of the truck, mostly because he left me to pull the suitcase all on my own and went trotting off to have a look.

The Tourist blustered into the house, stopping to open door after door and peer into the living room and the dining room and the kitchen, until Mum cornered him against the greeting desk, forced him to sign the book, and ushered him up the stairs.

"Lovely old farmhouse this. Beautifully preserved. Love what you've done with the paneling. Is this the original staircase? When do you serve dinner? Oh! Who am I standing on? What's your name?"

"Neil," I told him.

"These narrow corridors can be a bit tight, can't they?"

Mum was trying to squeeze past him to unlock the door to his room. He turned and nearly flattened her against the wall.

"Sorry!"

Dad and I carried his suitcases into the room, which had always been bright and airy, but now seemed dark and cramped with his huge body blocking all the light and dwarfing everything. Dad touched my elbow and made a gesture with his head, so we left Mum to settle our visitor and slipped away.

"Weathermen," mused Dad as we went down the stairs, "were not traditionally renowned for their hospitality, you know. By nature we tended to be closed off and secretive. Visitors were not encouraged. Travelers seeking shelter were not welcomed. Some Weathermen shrouded the fort in mist and rain all year round, which must have been a bit glum. One guy thought it was a good idea to embed the whole thing in a block of ice! He was frozen solid for a month and nearly didn't thaw out in time for the next ceremony. Never thought I'd be nostalgic for those times."

Instead of leading the winding way down to his study where I do most of my Learning the Awesome Responsibilities of Being the Weatherman, he went out through the front door and stood on the path and stared out over the wooded hill in front of our house.

"Can you feel it, Neil?" he said. "Can you feel it building up over there?"

I swallowed and stood up straight and tried to reach out with all my senses, to feel the weight of the air and the movement of things too small and light to be seen or touched, but whose shifting patterns fill the sky with avalanches and tidal waves. It's hard, sometimes, to tune into the elementals. It's like the trick with that picture that's a woman one minute and a rabbit the next. I can't always make myself see the one I'm looking for. But this time the dark cold mass building behind the hill was impossible to miss. I felt it like an angry chill running over my skin.

"What the heck is that?" I asked.

"Snowstorm," Dad replied. "Now, Weatherman, what are you going to do about a snowstorm in September?"

"Me?" I squeaked.

"What have I taught you, Neil? You have everything you need. Take your time. But hurry up, or we'll get snowed in on the last day of Summer!"

Yeah, so, what exactly had he taught me?

Liz and Owen and I had never gone to school. Mum and Dad had always taught us at home, because all the stuff I had to learn to be Weatherman couldn't be learned at school. When they tried to send Liz, she ran away and hid for two days, and when they tried to send Owen, he looked up at them with his big brown eyes and his lower lip all wobbly and they gave up on school for any of us altogether. So the two of them kept crowding into classes that were supposed to be just for the future Weatherman. They were learning all the stuff that was supposed to be secret Weatherman knowledge. Liz said it would save her the trouble of having to learn it all later when I turned out to be useless and she had to take over, and Owen was emergency backup Weatherman in case I went mad with jealousy and started a Weather War with Liz and we ended up destroying each other with giant tornadoes. Stuff like that is why you should never, ever listen to Liz.

Lesson one: how the weather works.

The skies are crowded. Honestly, they're just packed.

We call them the elementals, because they're, well, elements. They live in the sky and make the weather, and the things they do affect stuff like temperature and moisture and air pressure and who knows what else? (Hint: *I'm* supposed to know what else.) And when they clump together you get wind and rain and snow and heat and frost and fog and monsoons and squalls and everything else that is, you know, weather.

The big ol' sun does most of the work, heating things up and letting things cool, while elementals run around, doing their thing—mixing it up, making the weather, *being* the weather.

The winds that roar through our upper atmosphere you would not believe. Powering through the stratosphere, around the poles and across the tropics. Those winds used to be everywhere. Some could freeze you solid. Some could roast you in a flash. Some were full of dust that could strip you to the bone, and some were full of rain so hard and heavy that it could flatten you to a strip. Mostly you stayed in your cave and you didn't go out much. If you were lucky, the weather wouldn't scour everything edible off the face of the Earth while you were in there.

We were all going to die. All of us. Everything. There would have been a planet of nothing but rock and dust and water for the elementals to play with till the sun went nova.

Whoever the first Weatherman was, he (or she, Liz would say here) somehow saw the elementals and reached out to them and touched them and tried to talk to them—even though elementals don't talk, any more than the microbes in your bodies talk. But somehow that Weatherman pushed them together, made them cooperate—more and more of them clumping together, working together, until finally they became complex creatures that could take control. And the Weatherman could speak to it—and it could listen.

That first lonely, lost, amazing genius of a Weatherman saved us all. We owe that person everything. We have no idea who he was.

There were four of these creatures. We call them Seasons. Don't try to understand them. They're too big and powerful and alien, and they don't care about us. Except for one thing. Without that first Weatherman, they would not exist, and so they kind of owe us, and they pay us back every day by NOT sweeping us into the air and sending us flying around the top of the world for all eternity.

The Weathermen at the four corners of the world regulate the Seasons, ushering them through the Doorways, allowing the Seasons to change at the right times around the world, ensuring the weather doesn't spiral out of control and destroy us all. The Seasons don't just pass through the Doorways, they pass through the Weathermen, becoming part of them. Weathermen have the special and terrible power of last resort to bring a Season back into them and become that Season in all its might. It's supposed to be a safeguard in case a Season goes crazy and forgets the agreement, or against a truly planet-threatening threat. To use that power is a crime, no matter how justified, and the person who uses it can no longer be Weatherman and will probably be dead. The last time it happened the four Seasons came from the four quarters of the world to judge the Weatherman, and they were so disgusted and enraged they exiled him from the Earth. I think his body is still up there, in orbit somewhere between here and the moon.

The Seasons don't like it when anyone interferes with the weather at all, which is why the Weathermen almost never do, even though they can. Except when things get weird. It's Weatherman's work to wrestle Weird Weather, and though I was not the weather wrestler I was the weather wrestler's son and I'd have to wrestle weather until the weather wrestling's done.

The skies were crowded, so I felt my way into the crowd. I rose up through the top of my head, seeing my body standing next to Dad on the path below. I floated away from the house, out over the trees and the hill to Loch Farny and the farm beside it. Low over the lake, practically on top of it, I saw a heavy black cloud—the sort that's only supposed to form under certain conditions at certain times of the year. Not here and not now. I could hear Dad's voice beside me, guiding me. I could see down, down, down into the microscopic world where elementals were swarming and rushing. Wherever they went the wind blew, snow formed, clouds billowed, air froze. All those tiny things were joining together, building and swirling, working to make a cloud full of snow. I reached out to them. Dad showed me how. I touched them and changed them, I turned them and broke them up and sent them away.

Back you go to where you should be, I told them.

The cloud broke and the elementals scattered and the temperature rose. Something under the lake wailed and groaned, so faint and far away I might have dreamed it, but this wasn't dreaming.

"Dad," I said, sick and horrified for reasons I didn't understand. "Dad, there's something under the lake."

"It's OK," he said. "Come back now."

There was a rush and a sound like the flapping of wings, and I was back in my own body again.

"Dad," I began.

"Don't worry about it," Dad said. "I'll take care of it."

"Wow!" said a voice from behind us, and we whirled around to see Ed Wharton grinning at us from the open door. "Heightened sensory perception, extraphysical projection of consciousness, and fine-particle manipulation. I knew it!"

"Now, look here, Mr. Wharton," Dad said.

"Call me Ed!" he boomed. "So which one of you is the Weatherman?"

CHAPTER 4

LIZ

I leaped the ditch and ran along the tree trunk that had fallen across the wire fence years before. The trees swallowed me up, and I was safe and hidden. The woods are about a half a mile wide and a mile and a half long. There's a wide path for walkers that runs down the middle, but we mostly stayed off that and roamed and quested and fought through the twisty small paths and tracks, the hidden hollows full of ivy and ferns and the broken mossy walls.

Behind me the Tourist was bent over trying to gather up his stuff, and I heard the door open and the others come out. I knew I'd get into trouble for not staying to help him, but I was mad at him for sneaking up on me and mad at myself for being snuck up on. Nobody should be able to sneak up and startle a Shieldsman like that.

Neil and me, we used to play in the woods a lot. I'd be a Shieldsman and fight battles and defeat enemy armies and ninjas and monsters. He'd be the Weatherman and cast spells and fight witches and wizards and warlocks. We didn't play much anymore. Sometimes Owen would come into the woods with me but he was too little and annoying to be any good at those games.

Neil didn't think being the Weatherman was a game anymore. Well, neither was being a Shieldsman. He had his job to do. I had mine. All the Shieldsmen had vanished hundreds of years ago and the Weathermen's Club was nearly gone—the members blaming Dad for it, too, telling lies and things. So to heck with them. It was up to me and Neil now.

I was just crossing the big path when I heard footsteps coming down the hill.

The woods ran from the road to the big path, then up from the big path to the crown of the hill, and on the crown of the hill was a tall old wall. On the other side of the wall was enemy territory where we could not go. That was where the Fitzgeralds lived, on the shore of Loch Farny, in the house they stole from my grandfather. When you heard someone coming down from there it usually meant Hugh Fitzgerald was riding forth to do evil. It was not a good idea to meet Hugh Fitzgerald.

Good old horrible old Hugh. One year older than Neil.

Three years older than me. Tall, tall, tall—not to mention slim and golden-haired, with a face like an angel in an old painting, and every time he met us he beat us up. We didn't let him! We'd fight back or run away and, if it was Neil and me together, we'd sometimes very nearly almost kind of sort of win. Mostly it was just hitting and slapping and pulling hair, pushing us down, rolling us around on the ground with his foot while he laughed and said mean things. I'd gotten really good at hearing him coming and hiding and following without him knowing it.

I ducked off the path and behind a thick clump of nettles. I watched his back as it moved out of the shade into a patch of light and back into shade again. That was him—Hideous Hugh, light-dark, light-dark, all tangled in his own shadows. He had his mum's face and his dad's hair. He was lucky it wasn't the other way around, Neil always said, or they'd keep him in a kennel and teach him to round up sheep.

I drew myself in and went still, and cold shivers ran over me and through me. I'd been startled by the Tourist, and he'd made me jump and breathe fast. I was wary of Hugh because, while I'd fight him if I had to, I didn't want to. I preferred to practice my stalking on him instead.

But now I felt scared, really scared, because I'd suddenly realized something was stalking *me*.

I heard voices, high and cracked and old, like trees

creaking before they fall. I squatted down even farther behind my clump of nettles and tried to stop myself from shaking while Hugh stepped out onto the main path. Two toothless, bent old women, with bony faces and sharp chins, wearing dirty, raggedy dresses came up the big path, leaning on sticks but moving surprisingly fast. They called Hugh over to them.

Don't go, I thought. It seemed stupid. Why was I scared of two old women in the woods? So scared I was even worried for flipping Hugh?

The women were complete strangers to me. I had no idea who they were or where they'd come from. Sometimes buses brought groups of pensioners out here for walks along the big path, but these two looked older than anyone I'd ever seen on the path before. Their clothes and their hair and their skin were so dirty and worn and ragged they might have come out of ancient times, when old women lived wild in the woods and everyone kept clear of them because they said they were mad or witches or hags or mad-old-witch-hags, which is an absolutely disgraceful and horrible way to treat old women.

Except maybe not these old women.

"Have you seen our cat?" one of them asked Hugh.

Hugh stopped and stared at them. I could tell by his face he was more disgusted than scared. *Idiot, Hugh! Run while you can!*

24

"No," he said, and he stuck his hands in his pockets, hunched his shoulders and walked past them. One of them did something with her stick, and Hugh's foot flew up into the air like a high kick in a dance. He fell flat on his back with a cry and a groan. The old women whirled around him like savage birds.

"He tripped!" one said.

"He is clumsy," the other one added.

"Tripped over his own feet, the *craytur*."

"He has a nice singing voice."

"Sing us a song, little boy."

"About our cat."

"We're looking for our cat."

"Have you seen him?"

"Naughty cat."

"Sing again and he might come running."

They were standing over Hugh, one on either side. He was sitting up now, leaning on his elbow and trying to rub his back with his hand, his expression all puzzled and mad.

"Go away, you crazy old—"

One of the women, her crooked stick in her crooked hand, poked him in the stomach.

"Aaagh!" Hugh cried.

"That's it, sing!"

They were both poking him now. He was flat on his back, trying to fend them off. They must have been stronger than they looked. I should have been enjoying it, I suppose. I'd never seen anyone torment Hugh like that before, and God knows he deserved it, but something about the old women was so wrong and out of place I felt as if I were almost on Hugh's side, and I just wanted him to get away from them.

Please don't see me, I thought. *Please don't see me.*

"Here, kitty, kitty, kitty!" called one of the women.

Poke, poke, poke.

"Aaghaaghagh!" squawked Hugh.

"Louder! He can't hear you!"

At last Hugh rolled himself out of poking range. He groaned and clutched his stomach.

"Golden boy! Golden giant! Did you eat our cat?" demanded one of the women. "Will I poke you some more to see if he flies out of your mouth?"

She waved her stick at him with her left hand. The other one waved a stick with her right hand. They made for Hugh, sticks ready to poke. Then one of them stopped and pointed with her stick.

"I see him!" she screeched. "Over there!"

"Get him!"

"Bad cat!"

"Do you want the golden boy to eat you? Is that it?"

"He'll eat you! He'll eat you all up!"

Waving their sticks and screeching, the old women hobbled across the track, straight for my nettle patch. They stopped in front of it, and through the leaves I saw their scabby knuckles gripping their sticks and their hairy chins and their squinting eyes and knotted hair. I was taking tiny little breaths and my heart was beating like a rock that's hurrying down a mountain because it's late for an avalanche.

"That's not the cat! That's a dandelion!" one of them cried suddenly.

"Bad dandelion! Pretending to be our cat!"

And they whacked furiously at the dandelion, missing it completely and flattening a small bunch of ox-eye daisies.

Then suddenly they pushed their way through the nettles. I put my arms around my head, but they ignored me completely, brushing past me and knocking me over. I scrambled away from them and stumbled down onto the path. I slipped and went down on one knee. The old women were gone, their voices fading into the trees. I looked around and saw Hugh standing upright, face flushed, glowering furiously at me.

"Wow," I said. "Who were—"

"There you are," he interrupted. "I was looking for you."

"You were?" I got ready to run. I'd just watched Hugh get beaten up by two little old ladies. There was no way I was going to let him take it out on me.

"Well," he said. "Your brother, really, but you'll do. Tell him—"

"I'm not your messenger!"

"Shut up! It's important!"

"Important? A message to Neil from you, *important*? What is it? 'Next time I see ya, I'll fight ya'? That sort of thing?"

"No! God, why do you have to be so difficult? Just tell him to come to the lake, right? He's to come to the lake. There's something there for him."

"What, a beating?"

"No! Come on! This isn't me, this is Mum, right?"

"Your . . . your mum?"

"Yeah, so, you know, it's important."

I wasn't sure what to say to that. Why would Mrs. Fitzgerald want Neil to go to the lake? I was kind of surprised she even knew Neil existed.

"Fair enough," I said. "If it's important to you and your mum, then you can be absolutely sure and certain that there's no way in hell he'll ever come."

"He has to! We've been trying to get your old man to come all Summer, but he won't. Mum says Neil will do instead, and I'm supposed to—"

He stopped. The two old women must have shaken him up even more than I'd thought. Hugh was obviously supposed to get Neil up to Loch Farny, either by using some clever plan or by just twisting his arm behind his back and forcing him. Instead he'd blurted the whole thing out to me, and I saw him clench his teeth as he realized what he'd done.

"Dad?" I said. "Why do you want Dad?"

"Never mind," he said through gritted teeth. "Try this. You tell Neil I'll be waiting for him at the lake if he wants to get back at me."

"Back at you for what?"

And for the second time that day, someone took me completely by surprise. Hugh lunged at me, hands outstretched, and gave me an almighty shove that lifted me right off my feet and threw me off the road and into the dry, stony ditch. I landed on my back, and my legs went flying over my head, rolling me onto my front so that I was lying facedown, mouth full of dust and sharp pebbles, half in the ditch and half in a patch of nettles and briars. The breath had been knocked so far out of me it was probably a gentle sea breeze on a distant beach. I waited for it to come back, and, when it did, a whole lot of hurting came with it.

"Ah! Ah! Ah! Ow!"

There were nettle stings and briar scrapes all along my legs, bruises and cuts on my back, more on my front and my arms and hands. I was covered in yellow dust, my head was ringing and my eyes watered. I hobbled out of the ditch, climbing the side with tiny, stiff steps. With every step I vowed an unholy vengeance on Hugh, who must have slithered off home like the snake he was while I was having all that fun getting to know the bottom of the ditch.

"What happened to you?" Owen asked. He was standing on the big path, holding my bow and arrows, which I had dropped.

"Hugh," I spat, wiping my eyes clear. "Flipping Hugh Fitz*flipping*gerald happened to me. What the heck are you doing here?"

He held out the bow and arrows.

"You have to help," he said. "He's trapped and you have to get him out."

"Who?" I asked, waving the bow and arrows away. I could barely put up with the breeze blowing on me, I didn't want them knocking against my scrapes and bruises, too. "Who's trapped? Where?"

"I'm not sure. At the smoky barn."

"Owen," I said. "I need . . . I need to go . . . I can't . . ."

"Please," he said.

"Oh, for flip's sake, Owen."

We went slowly and carefully—me limping and groaning and grabbing clumps of dock leaves to rub on my nettle stings. There's a big wide boggy clearing called the Ditches next to the road, just up from our house. We crossed over the mud and the reeds and the goat willow and climbed onto the road. I nearly turned and headed for home. I wanted a cool shower and a soft bed, and maybe Mum to put cream on my cuts and bruises, and Dad to make me hot chocolate, and both of them to tell me I was an idiot but smiling while they did it.

"Come on!" said Owen. I thought of all the times Owen had tagged along and driven me crazy by going slow and dawdling and wandering off to look at a flower or a stick, and now it was his turn to get mad at me. "You have to hurry!"

"Go boil your head, Owen," I said, but I turned away from home and followed him down to the smoky barn.

The smoky barn was on the right, set just off the road with a big, overgrown clearing in front of it. It had burnt down years before when some boys had snuck in there to smoke cigarettes and ended up setting the whole thing on fire. It had never been rebuilt or repaired—it was just a big mess of bent and burnt and rusted metal, all covered in weeds growing through blackened piles of hay, and nobody ever went there, not even to smoke cigarettes. Now I could see that there was a great big truck and a big long trailer parked beside it, and banging on the side of the trailer with their sticks and screeching at the tops of their voices were the two old women who had tripped Hugh in the woods.

I grabbed at Owen, but he was just out of reach and he ran right at them.

"No! Owen!" I shouted after him.

"Cat!" said one old woman.

"Cat!" said the other.

"We know you're in there, cat!"

"Hiding!"

"Cowardly cat!"

"Baby cat!"

They stood side by side, whacking away with their bent, crooked, thorny sticks that must have been hard as iron. The trailer was ringing like a set of church bells, booming and clanging and donging. Something inside cried out in rage and bumped against the walls. The whole trailer rocked from side to side, and so did my head.

"Get out, cat!"

"Out! Out! Out!"

"Stop!" Owen cried, running toward them and waving his arms about.

"Owen!" I yelled, and went after him as fast as I could, which was not very fast because I was not at my best.

The women stopped screeching and lowered their sticks.

"Stop?" said one.

"Why stop?" said the other.

"Our stupid, lazy cat won't come out."

"Won't do what it's told!"

"Bad cat."

"No!" said Owen. "It can't! Look! Look!"

He pointed at the doors at the back of the trailer, which were held shut by a long metal lever. He dropped my bow and arrows and climbed up and grabbed the lever.

"Help me!" he said.

"Help him!" said one of the old women, pointing her stick at me.

I froze.

"Help him," said the other, jumping up and down with excitement.

If my bow and arrows had been in my hands instead of on the ground I might have used them, but I can't be sure it wouldn't have just made them mad. Madder.

Owen was pulling and tugging at the lever, gradually working it loose. I reached up with both hands, took hold of it, and pulled. It came away, the doors swung open, and a furry red elephant streaked out and yowled, then arched its back and hissed. The elephant was a cat, a cat the size of an elephant, an angry cat the size of an elephant with teeth and claws and blazing green eyes, and there we were, a pair of mice ready to be gobbled up.

It swiveled round, raised one paw, and crouched and stalked toward us. I had my bow picked up off the ground, an arrow nocked and drawn. I aimed for an eye—I knew I could hit it—and hoped it would be enough because I wouldn't get a second shot.

"Sssssh!" said Owen, and stepped into my line of sight.

"Owen!"

"It's OK!" Owen said, walking forward, hands up and out. "We won't hurt you! It's OK! Sssssshhhhh."

"OWEN!" I was screaming now. The cat crouched down low, mouth open wide, and slid straight at Owen, who reached up and tickled it under the chin.

"There," he said. "There. It's OK. There."

The cat tilted its head and closed its mouth, and Owen scratched behind its ear—an ear he could have walked into without bending over. The cat was sitting now, its tail waving, its eyes half closed, surprised and suspicious, but willing to be scratched. Owen kept whispering and hushing. He put his arms around its neck and buried his face in its fur.

Then things got weird, because the cat was suddenly in Owen's arms, his face still buried in its neck, but now it was the size of a normal cat, a tabby housecat. It was resting in Owen's arms, purring contentedly.

"He's hungry," Owen said. "I want to go home and give him something to eat."

"He was going to eat *us*!" I yelled.

"Well, he's not now," Owen said, and walked off, carrying the cat.

I looked around. The truck doors were swinging gently on their hinges. There was no sign of the old ladies. My arm was sore. Every part of me was sore. My head swam and my knees shook, so I put the arrow away and the bow on my shoulder and followed Owen.

We went back to the house. Mum and Dad and Neil and the Tourist were all standing on the path in front of the door. They seemed to be having some sort of argument. Mum saw Owen and the cat first, because they were ahead of me.

"What the hell is that?" she groaned.

"It's a cat," said Owen with a bright, happy smile. "His name is Neetch!"

"It's a magic cat," I said, coming up behind him. "It was in the back of a truck down by the old barn. It was really, really big, and then it got small. There were two old women there, too. I think they might be living in the woods."

"Liz!" exclaimed Mum. "Oh my God, are you OK?"

"What happened?" Dad asked. "Did you fall?"

"There was a ditch," I said. "And some nettles and things. And I want to sit down now please."

"Holy Moses," Neil said. "Liz, was it—"

"A ditch," I repeated firmly.

"So," said the Tourist with a nervous laugh, holding his hands in front of him, his fingers wriggling together like fat worms dancing, his face pale and sweaty, his eyes wide. "You, uh, met the ladies and the bog beast, did you? And, ah, is everything OK? Nobody hurt too badly, I hope? No-body . . . turned into anything? Er . . . or . . . was eaten?"

I glared at him, but Mum and Dad ushered me indoors and Owen went off to find a can of salmon for the stupid cat and Neil followed, looking thoughtful and worried. The Tourist stood outlined in the doorway, his arms by his sides, his hands in fists, staring out at the trees, his face serious, his eyes narrowed. Then I was pushed into the living room and down onto the sofa, and creams and hot chocolate were applied, and Mum and Dad told me I was an idiot, but they smiled when they said it.

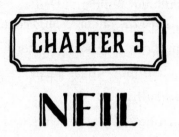

CHAPTER 5

NEIL

By the time Liz and Owen ran up, looking like they'd been fighting in a war and having amazing adventures rescuing cats from trees or whatever, we'd been standing on the path arguing for about ten minutes after the Tourist asked which of us was the Weatherman.

"Uh," Dad had said. "What?"

"Weatherman!" The Tourist had rolled out of the doorway toward Dad, arms spread wide, the delighted smile on his face making his beard dance and twitch. "Can I just say what a pleasure and an honor it is to be here, and what a rare privilege it is to watch you work—a master craftsman and his apprentice! *You*, sir, I take it are the Weatherman himself, one of the four caretakers of the world, honoring the ancient agreement between humanity and the Seasons, bringing order out of chaos and protecting us from their wrath?"

He had then looked at me.

"And you must be the junior Weatherman? Weatherman Junior? Weatherboy? I'm sorry, I don't know what a Weatherman-in-training calls himself."

"Neil," I said, dully.

Then Mum came out to see what was going on. The Tourist turned to her with both hands spread.

"Ah! You must be Mrs. Weatherman!"

Mum stopped, and glared.

"Excuse me, Mr. Wharton, I don't appreciate—" she began.

"Oh, I do beg your pardon—" the Tourist said.

"Just a minute, Mr. Wharton, could you—" Dad put in. And then everybody started talking at once . . .

". . . not a flippin' Weatherboy," I said.

". . . deserve a little respect and if you could . . ."

". . . meant no offense and spoke without thinking . . ."

". . . would very much like to know how you came by the information . . ."

". . . I mean everyone just assumed . . ."

". . . can't just come waltzing into our home and speak to us . . ."

". . . getting off on the wrong foot here . . ."

". . . not common knowledge, and your casual attitude . . ."

". . . nobody asked me if I wanted . . ."

". . . overfamiliar and frankly intrusive . . ."

". . . if you could just give me a chance . . ."

This went on and on and would have kept going on if Owen hadn't run up holding a cat followed by Liz, looking as if she'd been dragged through a hedge backward. She was coated in dust and covered in cuts, and there were horrible rashes all over her legs. She said something about falling, a ditch and nettles, but she looked at me for a moment, then away, and I knew she must have had help in her falling.

The Tourist, despite his size, somehow faded away into the background while Liz was put on the couch and Mum got cream and Dad went to make hot chocolate. Owen brought in his new cat and filled a bowl from a can of salmon. It ate noisily. Had Liz said something about it being a magic cat? I shook my head. Must be one of her silly games. Owen sat on the floor and stared up at her with his big, round, worried eyes until she let him climb up and snuggle in beside her.

"Neil," she said when Mum and Dad had left the room. "Don't—"

"We can't let him get away with it," I said. "You'd do the same if he did that to me."

"Yeah, but no, but listen! He said something about him and his mum wanting you to go up to the lake. Well, they want Dad, but they can't make him go, so they said you'd do. So this is just to make you go up, you see? It's a trap or something."

All the protective, big-brotherly blood that was normally neglected and unemployed—probably in a sad, sulky little pool way down in the tip of my big toe—had by now rushed in a suicidal charge straight to my head, but it wasn't just that. The lake! I remembered the thing under the water. There was something under the lake. Something that had tried to make a snowstorm, and had probably made all the other crazy weather this year.

"No," I told her. "It's OK."

Half of me was raging at Hugh, half of me was remembering that strange voice from under the water. All of me was up and out the door before Liz could get another word in. I crossed the road, went into the woods, and climbed the hill until I reached the wall. Then I climbed the wall and crossed into enemy territory.

On the shore of Loch Farny is our grandfather's farm, where the Fitzgeralds have lived for twenty years since they stole it away, and where we don't go. There's bad blood there, between us all.

Before the Seasons started arriving through our phone box, they used to come through a well on what was once

my grandfather's farm. Tobar Farny, the well was called—
the Well of Rain—a pool of sweet, pure water that lay
under a few limestone boulders in the middle of a field.
That field and that well had been in my family for thousands of years. That well was one of the four corners of the
world. Then Hugh's lousy dad, John-Joe Fitzgerald, persuaded my grandfather to invest in a new pub. My grandfather had no interest in pubs or investments, but John-Joe
had befriended Granddad after Granny died and he begged
Granddad to get the money for him. And Granddad, being
a good friend, took out a mortgage against his farm.

There was no pub. The money vanished. Granddad
could not manage the repayments. In his pride and shame,
he never asked the Weathermen's Club for help. Everything
happened with sickening speed.

The bank took Granddad's farm, put it up for sale, and
it was bought for a song by John-Joe. Granddad and Dad
were kicked out. John-Joe and his young wife moved in.

John-Joe drove a hired digger across his new field while
his wife watched. When he reached the pool, he extended
the arm of the digger and began gouging great chunks of
earth out from under the boulders. That was when the
water began to flow. A few hours later, Fitzy was left sitting on the roof of the digger, calling for help, surrounded
by the waters of a brand-new lake. Loch Farny, they call it
now—the Lake of Rain.

I went over the wall and down the hill to the edge of the trees in a white-hot fury. It was a fight I couldn't win, but that wasn't the point. Even if you lose a fight, you can do enough damage to make the other person sorry they started it and not likely to start another—if you're in the right mood.

There was the field and the lake and the farm, all pretty as a picture, the digger long gone. I stared at the lake for a long, slow moment. It was small, round, and not very deep. Nothing moved on the water.

There was no sign of Hugh. Flippin' Hugh—he wanted me here, didn't he? This was his idea of a clever trap? The best idea that moron could come up with! Well, here I was and—typical Hugh—he was too stupid to turn up for his own ambush!

I waited. My breathing slowed. My roaring, growling, snarling voice grew quiet, and my small, worried, sensible voice began asking what the heck I was doing here. Even thinking of my poor little sister and her stings and cuts didn't make me angry again, just sad. I knew me fighting Hugh wouldn't make her feel one little bit better.

Somewhere between the angry thoughts getting quieter and the worried thoughts getting louder, I began to hear a voice that wasn't mine—thin and faint, wordless and sad, desperate and lonely—calling for help. I left the trees and crossed the field to the edge of the lake. The voice grew louder. I couldn't help myself. I took off my shoes and socks, stripped down to my underpants, and waded into the lake.

Everything that happened next might as well have been happening to someone else because I felt as if I was watching it all from a long way away. I dived under the water and started to swim.

I swam down, down, down. The water was clear as crystal, though there wasn't much to see—just flat mud and scraps of weed and, toward the center, a pile of stones, even and regular like a cairn on a mountaintop, coated in slime and mud. There was a gap like a door, all black and shadowy, and in that door was a hand, reaching for me. The voice was growing louder all the time.

Without thinking, I reached out as if to shake hands. It was a funny-looking hand, thin and gray—more like the end of a branch of a tree at twilight—but it closed around mine like a living hand and held me tight.

The moment the hand touched mine, everything changed. It was like when Dad let me help him with the weather, only different, more intense, deeper somehow. But I had no breath left. My chest was on fire. And the hand would not let me go.

"Air," I begged the voice. "Make me air." And my lungs immediately filled without me breathing. There was so much air, it threatened to pop my poor sore chest like a balloon and I had to breathe out in a stream of bubbles. "Slow down!" I told the voice. "Take it easy!"

The hand squeezed tighter, the arm stopped above the elbow, the rest hidden under the rocks. Whatever the hand belonged to, the rest of it was trapped, and it wanted me to set it free.

"Sorry," I gasped, my voice funny in the water. "I don't know how."

The gray hand squeezed mine again, gentle, insistent. So maybe if I . . .

What could I do? I could roll away the rocks, but it was hardly the rocks that were the problem. This had been a Doorway, but the Doorway had been moved, and somehow this thing had been left trapped, half in and half out of a Doorway that was no longer there. But *some* of the Doorway must still be there, I figured, some tiny part that was holding the poor thing tight.

I had to do what Dad did. I had to open the Doorway, just a little, just a crack.

Could I do it?

I thought about what happens when a Season passes through a Doorway—the Weatherman and the Season become one. For that moment the Season gives up its power and hands it to the Weatherman as a token of honor and trust. And then the Weatherman hands it back.

So I reached out to the thing. I *became* the thing—

imprisoned for twenty years when it should have been roaming the skies. Anger and fear. I saw a tall dark shadow through the surface of the water, standing on the edge of the lake, and that shadow sent dark thoughts down, thoughts of chains and knots and cages. The bottom of the lake was a prison. The sky above was freedom. Between the lake and the sky was someone who wanted to enslave it for all time. The thing was young, and the thing wanted to get away from the terrible person who wanted to control it. It had cried out for help and rescue.

And I had come.

It was easy—like raising a chair leg to free the hem of a coat, and then letting it back down. The thing was free, and the trap was sprung.

The hand opened wide and let me go. I rose up surrounded by bubbles and clouds of dirt. I saw a thin gray shape rise up next to me and I heard the voice let out a scream.

Then my head broke the surface and I could breathe normally again.

I paddled wearily to shore and crawled out of the lake on all fours, my chest heaving, my lungs and throat burning, reaching for my clothes. There was no sign of the Gray Thing, but John-Joe Fitzgerald and his wife stood on a rise between me and the farm, looking at me. John-Joe just glared at me with poison and hate. Mrs. Fitzgerald was looking at the farm. I wiped my eyes and saw Hugh dragging something long and thin and dripping through the farm gate, like he was bringing the world's least Christmassy Christmas tree home for Christmas. Mrs. Fitzgerald glanced back at me.

"See him on his way," she told John-Joe, and started after Hugh.

John-Joe grinned down at me.

"A quick boot up the backside'll hurry you up," he said, and came toward me.

CHAPTER 6

LIZ

I'd had my quick cool shower and my creams and my hot chocolate, but I wasn't able to enjoy any of them properly because I was worrying about stupid Neil. It wasn't having a fight with Hugh that worried me, because if it were just a fight it wouldn't have been so bad. But it wasn't just a fight. It was Mrs. Fitzgerald. She wanted Neil. More to the point, she really wanted Dad, but would settle for Neil. That was bad.

I was back on the couch and Mum and Dad were telling me I was an idiot when Dad looked around and said, "Where's Neil got to? His hot chocolate's going to get cold."

"He went up to the lake because Hugh pushed Liz into a ditch and told her his mum wanted you to go up to the lake but Neil would do instead," Owen said.

I glared.

"Sneak," I said.

Owen did that thing where he turns his head a bit as if he's looking back over his shoulder at whatever he just said or did to see what he'd done wrong this time. His eyes went wide and his face fell.

"Sorry!"

Dad had stood up and was looking down at me very seriously. I could see him thinking about giving out to me and telling me what I'd done wrong and that I was an idiot but without the smiles this time. He swallowed it all down.

"I'm going to go get him. Stay here."

I said I couldn't do that because I was going, too, only I didn't say it out loud because that way he would have heard me and said no. Instead I stared at the carpet as if I was properly ashamed of myself. Mum and Owen followed him to the front door, and I hopped off the couch and went out the back and around. Dad got his bike out of the shed and cycled away, turning left down the road, and when Mum and Owen went back indoors I got on my bike and cycled after him.

Dad went fast, standing on the pedals the whole way, and I could barely keep up with him. Even with the shower and the creams and the dock leaves, I was still sore and weary, but he was in such a hurry he never looked behind.

The tiny old road up to the farm was muddy and rocky and broken enough to wreck a bike, rider and all. The gate was off the hinges and lying against the hedge. Dad got off and walked, and so did I. He must have heard my bike rattling on the rocks, because he stopped and turned, looking exasperated.

"Liz," he said. "Go home."

I shook my head. We stood there for a while, neither of us going anywhere.

"OK," he said at last, "but stay back."

We came up to the house. There was a big barn across from it and a wide yard between full of weeds. At the other end was the gate that led into the field and the lake, and through the open gate came Neil, tripping over his own feet, wearing nothing but his underpants, shivering, hair plastered to his head, lips blue with the cold, body smeared with mud and grass. He was trying to hold on to his clothes, which kept falling out of his hands and his arms. Behind him, roaring and cursing and waving his fists and kicking at him with his big wellies caked in cow dung, came John-Joe Fitzgerald.

"WHAT THE HELL DO YOU THINK YOU'RE DOING?" Dad roared. I'd never heard Dad use his Big Voice on another grown-up before. Somehow it sounded even bigger when he did.

"Uh, suh-sorry, Duh-dad, I juh-just—"

"Oh, not you, Neil, YOU, you big thug! GET AWAY FROM HIM!"

"Trespassin' and poachin' on me land!" barked John-Joe, waving a finger in the air but keeping Neil between him and Dad. "Thinks he can come down and go for a swim on me lake as if he owns it! I'll have the cops on him, I will! On the lot of ye!"

"Cops, my eye, you'll be lucky if I don't have you up for assault!" Dad told him. Then he knelt beside Neil and began to help him dress, all the time scolding John-Joe who was doing a hopping dance, forward and backward, making more threats and accusing Neil of rustling, burglary, and tax dodging.

I clenched my fists and took a step forward, ready to get between Neil and John-Joe and scream at him till his eardrums burst, but then an odd movement in the barn caught the corner of my eye. I do not know to this day how anything in the world could have distracted me from the sight of Neil and Dad and John-Joe, but I turned, and then I crossed the yard to get a better look.

The barn was full of broken wood, rotting and crumbling, and choked with dock weed and thistle and ragwort. Behind the wood was Hugh. He had a stick. He was hitting something on the floor.

Everyone's always amazed at how good-looking Hugh is. They wonder how his Dad could have a son like that. But I think he looks just like his Dad sometimes—when he looks down his nose at something with those animal eyes, his mouth hanging open, showing his teeth. He's not so good-looking then.

I was slow and quiet coming around the piles of wood. There was a thing on the ground, gray and blue, thin as thread, curled up, hugging itself. I forgot that I was hiding. I forgot to be afraid of Hugh.

"What are you doing?" I said.

Hugh turned on me, raising the stick, face twisted. He stopped, eyes wide.

"What the hell are you doing here?" he demanded.

I looked past him.

"What is that?" I asked. It lowered its arm and I saw two eyes like angry black slashes on its narrow face. The air shimmered around it with a golden glow and something rattled on the roof of the barn. White hailstones fell through the holes and shattered on the ground around us.

"Stupid!" yelled Hugh, swinging the stick at the gray-blue thing. "Stop! Stupid!"

I jumped to grab the stick, missed, but caught Hugh's wrist with both hands and twisted. But he was too strong and I was too small. His arm wouldn't move. He grabbed at my hands with his free hand, and I put all my weight on his wrist, nearly pulling him over. I lifted both my feet and kicked my heels into his stomach. There wasn't much force behind it, to be honest, but it made him double over and his face went red and he dropped me then the stick and staggered backward a bit, clutching himself, looking astonished.

More hailstones fell. The golden glow spread.

"NO!" Hugh, panicking, reached for the stick. I picked it up and waved it at him. He crouched down with his arms spread and started circling. I held the stick two-handed over my head, in a samurai-fighting stance. My feet were slipping and crunching on hailstones the size of golf balls, and more were bouncing wildly around us, flashing in the golden light.

A dark shadow blocked out the light. The golden glow went out. A figure crouched low over the thing on the floor and touched it, and the thing whimpered and curled up like a drowned spider.

"Leave it alone!" I tried to shout, but it came out as a croak. Suddenly all my aches and pains and stings started to burn, and I closed my eyes and dropped the stick and felt tears pour from my eyes and heard myself groan.

A cool hand touched my cheek and all the pain went away.

I opened my eyes to see a face, pale and beautiful, dark hair framing gray eyes and blue lips. I recognized Mrs. Fitzgerald. She smiled at me.

"You must be Liz," she said.

"Mum?" said Hugh.

"Be quiet, Hugh. Go check on your father."

She rested a hand on my shoulder and held me until I was steady on my feet.

"Thank you," I said. Her smile did not change. She stood between me and the thing on the floor. I didn't dare try to look around her. Sunlight shone in a beam through the hole in the roof. The broken ice of the hailstones was melting away into shrinking puddles.

"There," she said. "It's finally done, and now I can begin."

"What?" I said. "What is that thing on the ground?"

"The future," she said. "And whoever owns it, owns the future. Everything is going to change now, Liz. You must prepare yourself. The future is mine.

"I think you and your father and brother should go now. You might think about telling them what you've seen in here, but that would force a confrontation and it's too early for that. Your father still has a job to do, doesn't he? It's the last day of Summer. Season's end. Tomorrow will bring a whole new world."

She closed her eyes and raised a finger and the barn was filled with the rushing, whispering hiss of a gentle breeze.

"LIZ!"

I jumped at Dad's shout and blinked.

"Here! Here!"

I backed away from Mrs. Fitzgerald, and she kept pace with me as I stepped backward out of the barn and into the yard.

"Liz, are you OK?"

"Yeah," I said. It was hard to turn my back on her but I had to get Dad and Neil out of there. In a day of shocks and shoves and frights and fear, I knew that the worst danger in the world was in that barn and in that woman. "Come on, let's get out of here. Let's go!"

Dad looked confused, and gave Mrs. Fitzgerald a puzzled glance. Neil was dressed and looking soggy and sorry and defeated. John-Joe had his hands on his hips and his lower lip stuck out and the toe of his left boot was tapping impatiently. Hugh had tilted his chin up so he could sneer properly down his nose at us.

"OK," Dad said, and he waved us both out of the yard ahead of him, and we walked our bikes back down the narrow road. I let Neil cycle mine, and Dad sat me up on his crossbar. The farther we got from the farm, from the thing, from *her*, the safer I should have felt. But I didn't. The closer we got to home, the more the sense of danger grew, and somehow I knew that today had been a bad day, but tomorrow was going to be even worse.

CHAPTER 7

NEIL

The cycle home from Loch Farny was one of the most horrible, uncomfortable, disgusting things I have ever had to go through. My clothes were wet and cold because I didn't have anything to dry myself with before putting them back on. They stuck to me and got into corners and itched and scraped and chafed until I thought I'd go mad. Worse than that, Liz's bike was too small for me and my knees were sticking out and it was almost too hard to pedal and I was so tired and the road just went on and on and I thought it would never end, and then it did, and I wished it hadn't.

I was in trouble. Liz was in trouble. The Tourist was in trouble. Even Owen was in trouble because he kept bringing the cat into the house. Liz and I kept trying to explain in different ways that Mum and Dad were in trouble, too, though we couldn't exactly say how or why, only that it had to do with the Tourist, the cat, the old women in the woods, the Fitzgeralds, the thing in the lake and the other thing in the barn—oh, no, wait, I think that must have been the same thing.

But Mum and Dad were having a hard time just dealing with me going off and jumping in the lake and with Liz sneaking off to follow Dad when he went to rescue me from jumping in the lake.

I showered and changed my clothes and had something to eat, and the whole time they were interrogating me to within an inch of my life, until I broke down crying and begged them to stop. Then they got embarrassed and said they were sorry and Liz muttered that I was a softy, but we both knew if it hadn't been me it would have been her.

Mum and Dad brought out the picnic table and chairs and set them up on the lawn. I got the broken one that creaked when you moved. We sat in the rosy glow of the evening, insects rising from the grass and crows flocking to roost.

Dad made me go through what I'd seen and done under the lake for the millionth time. Then he made Liz go through what she'd seen in the barn for the million and *oneth* time. She kept adding stuff about two mad old women in the woods and something about Owen's cat, which she seemed to think was important, and I reminded him of the

Tourist turning up out of nowhere and knowing stuff, and how it all added up to . . . something. Dad didn't argue, but he didn't look entirely convinced, either.

Mum was like a black cloud, glowering and staring, her eyes flashing with far-off bursts of lightning. She listened to me and Liz, glaring at the hill beyond the road as if daring the monsters hidden there to take one step closer. The monsters stayed in hiding, which was just as well for them.

Owen and his cat, well, kitten, actually—I could have sworn it was bigger earlier—were playing on the grass with a piece of paper tied to some string. At least someone was having a good time. Liz was sitting in a chair next to me, half listening to the interrogation and half watching Owen and the kitten intently—as if one of them was going to grow fangs or something.

Dad sat back in his chair and crossed one leg over the other and rubbed his chin. He was frowning, and his face looked worn and worried and haunted.

"The thing under the lake has been sending strange weather to us all Summer. I think it was trying to get our attention. After the first few times, I knew something would have to be done, but I couldn't risk doing it alone. I've been trying to contact the Weathermen's Club for the last two months. I've phoned, e-mailed, written letters. No response. They've either vanished from the face of the Earth or they're sulking because I haven't tried to get in touch with them since . . . well, since I became Weatherman. I'm a bit worried."

"Couldn't you just go to them?" I asked.

Dad made a face.

"We Weathermen don't travel," he said. "It's not a rule, exactly, but there's a strong taboo against going farther than a few miles from the Doorway. It looks like I'll have to, though, doesn't it? I've been putting this off too long. Tomorrow, when the Autumn has arrived, I'll see about getting a lift to the train."

I nodded. No farther than a few miles? As the future Weatherman, I did not really like the sound of that.

"We've always known there's something . . . off about Mrs. Fitzgerald," Dad said. "We've stayed well away from her. Now it turns out we were right and we should have been more on our guard. Mrs. Fitzgerald wanted the thing free from the lake. For some reason only the Weatherman or his heir could do it. My guess is that though she couldn't get at it, she must have scared it somehow. It became desperate and reached out to me—to the Weatherman—in the only way it could. Now she's captured it, and God knows what she's going to do next."

I blushed furiously and sank deeper into my chair. It creaked loudly.

"So what is it?" said Liz. "Is it an elemental?"

Dad shook his head.

"No. And yes. It can control the weather, but it seems more aware than a simple elemental. I don't know what else it can be, though."

"But, Dad," I said, an odd feeling inside me, a sick-scared-excited feeling. "It was trapped in the Doorway. It was trapped *by* the Doorway. It must have been going through the Doorway when the Doorway was moved and it got caught. Simple elementals don't move through the Doorways, Dad."

"No," said Dad. "They don't."

"Is it a Season?" asked Liz, seeing as no one else was going to come out and actually say it.

"It can't be," I said.

"You opened the Door for it," Mum said. "You merged with it. What was it like?"

"It all happened too fast," I told her, remembering that shimmering image of the tall shadow standing beside the lake. "It was scared and angry and sick of being under there, but mostly it was afraid of what was waiting for it."

"Mrs. Fitzgerald," said Liz.

"Sounds to me," said Ed Wharton, "as if we've got a new Season. Five Seasons. How about that? What'll we call it?"

Everything was blue and dark in the twilight cool. Ed was leaning casually against the corner of the house, arms and legs crossed. Bats flew around the eaves over his head. Or maybe his beard came to life at dusk and went hunting for food. He straightened and before anyone could challenge him for eavesdropping under the eaves, he pointed at Neetch.

"Great googly moogly! Do you know what that is? It's the Bog Beast of Moherbeg! How come he didn't eat you? He usually eats people he doesn't like, and he doesn't like *any*body."

"He did *try* to eat us," said Liz. "But he was . . . bigger at the time."

"Bigger?" I said.

"Much bigger."

"Well, he likes me, and I like him," Owen said. "His name is Neetch."

"Neetch?" asked Ed Wharton.

"Neetch," said Owen.

Ed Wharton looked at Owen and lowered his beard to his chest and intoned solemnly.

"Son, the Bog of Moherbeg looks down on the towns and villages of three counties, where people lock their doors and fasten their windows at night, not for fear of burglars, but for fear of that terrible thing!"

Neetch had rolled on his back with the string tangled in his paws.

"Mothers warn their children not to go out after dark, and threaten them with the bog beast when they're bold. People lie awake at night shivering under their blankets in terror of his shadow falling over them when he pads across their moonlit lawns. There isn't a dog in twenty miles that isn't kept tied up in the kitchen every night! And you *like* him?"

"He's misunderstood," said Owen.

"And *he* likes *you*?"

"We just get on well," Owen said and shrugged. "I'm not mean to him like everyone else is."

Dad had stood up when Ed Wharton had first spoken, and he and Mum closed in on either side of the Tourist now, their faces grim. He smiled nervously at them.

"Mr. Wharton," Mum said. "Perhaps you could explain yourself."

"Explain? Explain what? I'm just a tourist."

"You're no more a tourist than I am the Pope," Dad said. "You know about the Weathermen. You had a bog beast in your trailer in the shape of a kitten—"

"Much bigger!" interrupted Liz. "And the old hags! They said the cat was theirs, so he must know about them, too!"

"Oh, now, please," Ed said. "Don't let them hear you call them that!"

"I'll call 'em what I like!" Liz grumbled.

"Shush!" he said. "They'll hear!"

"You are incredibly lucky," Mum said softly, "that none of our children were hurt. Sit down and explain yourself, Mr. Wharton. Then we will decide what to do with you."

Even in the fading light I could see his face turn red. Head bowed he sat on a lawn chair that creaked under his weight, even though it wasn't cracked.

"Look," he said. "You have absolutely nothing to worry about. All I want to do is watch the ceremony! I want to see the Autumn arrive! That's all."

"There isn't much to see," Dad told him.

"Of course not. These things occur on several different levels. Sight is not the only sense! Anyway, just to be there when it happens . . . that's enough! You see, I *am* a tourist. I travel the world, seeking wonders and marvels to behold—but not just any wonders and marvels! Not the Leaning Tower of Pisa or the Grand Canyon or the Taj Mahal. I seek secret wonders, *hidden* wonders!

"When I was a little boy, no older than Owen, there, I wanted to be a magician. Not the sort that pulled rabbits out of hats and did card tricks on stage. I wanted to have power. Power to crack the earth! Part the seas! Pull the stars down to a mountaintop and command them to dance! I left school early, lied about my age, and got a job driving trucks. That took me all over the world. I read books, I talked to people and, slowly but surely, I tracked down magic, real magic. A cottage in the Black Forest. A stone on the Russian steppes. An oasis in the Sahara. Magic places guarded by magic folk! I visited these places and I discovered two things. One was that I would never be a magician. I have no talent for magic. None. But I do have a nose for it. That was the second thing. I had a talent for finding magic, and that's what I do. I find magic."

"And when you find it?" Mum asked.

Ed Wharton smiled and shrugged.

"What do tourists do? We experience it. We witness it. We remember it. And then we bore people to tears telling them crazy stories about it that they never believe. So, on the morning of the twenty-first, all I will do is stand back and watch and enjoy. Then I'll shake your hands and pay my bill and be on my way. And—who knows?—you might even have me back next year!"

"And that would be fine," Dad said, "but I'd like to know how you got here and why you brought a bog beast with you."

"And two old women!" Liz put in.

"And two old women," Dad agreed.

Ed Wharton tapped his fingers nervously on the table.

"It was a story I heard, you see, from an old Irish laborer I met at a bus stop in south London. He'd emigrated when he was twelve and worked on the building sites his whole life. Never went home. What money he didn't send to his family, he drank away. He told me his granny used to say that there were three old women, sisters, who guarded a black pool up in the mountains in Ireland, living in the shell of a giant snail. They stirred the pool with their sticks and sang songs. The stirring was to keep the thing in the pool awake; the singing was to keep it calm. If the thing ever slept, the whole world would go out. If the singing stopped, the thing would get mad and climb out of the pool and knock the land into the sea.

"When I was back in Ireland I tracked the sisters down. I discovered their giant snail shell, turned to rock long ago, deep in a bare mountain hollow—but there were only two of them, along with their pet bog beast, who chased me round the mountain a few times before picking me up in its mouth and carrying me back to the shell. They said that one day their sister had stopped her singing and her stirring and told them she was going outside to have a look at the sun. They begged her not to, but out she went and she never came back.

"By the time I found them, their sister had been gone a long time. At first they'd been worried about her. They missed her terribly. Then they got mad at her for abandoning them and leaving them to stir and sing alone. They told me all this themselves, taking turns to sing while the other one talked, though they were constantly interrupting each other. So I fixed up their shell a little, mended a few holes, put in a bit of dry lining and insulation, laid down a proper floor, and put in a few scraps of furniture and a stove. I brought them some pasta and, er, chorizo and canned goods and stuff.

"They'd taken their miserable existence for granted until I introduced them to a few home comforts. Now their shell is waterproof, insulated, has a water boiler and electricity, and they get regular deliveries from the local supermarket.

"On my last visit they'd decided they'd had enough. Their sister was out and about having a great time, leaving them to look after the black pool and they were sick of it. They decided to go look for her. I wasn't sure it was a good idea, but they said if they didn't do it now they'd never be able to do it. I don't really know what they meant by that but, anyway, we plugged in a CD player and put a disc of last year's Top Ten hits on repeat, and they put a spell on some sticks so they'd stir the pool by themselves, and then they got into my truck—it took ages to get the bog beast in—and off we drove.

"They told me where to find you, and all about the Weathermen, and they said that while they were finding their sister I could relax for a few days and see the Autumn arrive, and then we'd all head back. So, you see, it's all quite simple really!"

When he finished, we sat in silence. Full night had fallen. A million billion stars had come out. None of them cared about us or what we said or did, but still it made me feel better to see them all up there, twinkling seriously, as only stars can.

"What about the man?" Owen said.

"The man?" asked Ed Wharton.

"The laborer who told you the story. What happened to him?"

Ed Wharton said nothing for a moment. He turned his head very slightly so he was looking down at the grass and not at us.

"He, uh. He was dead, I'm afraid. He'd frozen to death at that bus stop one night years before. After we talked, I put his ghost in a bottle and I brought him back to Ireland and buried him next to his granny. He just wanted to go home. He wanted to lie down and rest under the mountains where he was raised."

Owen nodded thoughtfully, then looked up at Mum and Dad.

"The Tourist is OK," he said. "Let him stay."

Mum and Dad looked at each other.

"OK," Mum said.

"OK," Dad said.

I was staring at Ed Wharton, thinking about what he'd told us. Everything was swirling around in my head, and even though it was crazy, when the thought surfaced I just said it out loud.

"Is Mrs. Fitzgerald their sister?"

Ed stared thoughtfully back at me. "How old is she?" he asked.

"She looks as if she's in her late twenties," Mum said.

"She's looked like that since I was Neil's age, when I first saw her," Dad added.

Ed Wharton lifted his head to look at the stars, moving his lips silently, as if counting them all.

"Yeah," he said finally. "It's possible."

Mum and Dad looked at each other for a very long time. Finally Mum gave a nod.

"If her sisters want her to go home with them, maybe we should help them out. If she's stirring and singing to a black pool in a giant snail shell, she can't very well be bothering us, can she?"

"Mum," said Liz, "I don't think they're very nice."

"We don't want nice," Mum said. "Nice is the opposite of what we need."

"Yeah," Dad said heavily. He sighed, and, for some reason, looked over at me.

"We need the club, if it still exists," he said, and paused. "And we need the Shieldsmen, too."

"Dad—" I began, but Liz had jumped to her feet and was doing one of her dances.

"Yes, yes, yes! The Shieldsmen! We need the Shieldsmen, yes, we need the Shieldsmen!"

"First priority is the Autumn," Dad said. "Then . . . well, then . . ."

His shoulders slumped, and he looked tired and depressed and worried, and so did Mum.

"Mr. Wharton," she said. "I'll understand if you want to leave—with a full refund, of course . . ."

"No, no, no," said Mr. Wharton heartily, shaking his head. "Not at all. Wouldn't dream of it."

". . . but perhaps we could ask a favor of you."

"My dear lady, anything, anything at all."

"Would you take my husband to Dublin tomorrow? After the ceremony, when the Autumn is safely here."

"To Dublin?"

"To the Weathermen's Club."

Mr. Wharton pursed his lips.

"And, uh, would I be allowed to enter the club itself? As an escort? A bodyguard? A guest?"

Mum shrugged and looked at Dad.

"Mm? Oh, yes, I'm sure. I'm sure, yes . . ." he trailed off. Mr. Wharton beamed.

"It would be my pleasure, then! My absolute pleasure!" He clapped his hands with delight.

"Can I go? Can I go?" Liz danced and whirled in front of Dad, and he held up his hands and waved her quiet.

"We'll see, we'll see!"

"What about tonight?" I asked. "What about tomorrow? What about the Autumn?"

Dad looked grim.

"We're on our own. That'll have to do for now."

That was not a very cheerful thought to go to bed on,

but go to bed on it we did. We put the creaking plastic furniture away, decided to leave any washing up till tomorrow, hugged and kissed and told each other everything would be fine, and went to our rooms. I crawled under the covers and started to dream . . .

Something was stalking me through the house. I stumbled over furniture and fell down stairs as though everything familiar had been altered and rearranged. The whole house felt strange and foreign and something that hissed and growled was sometimes before me, sometimes behind me, sometimes above me and sometimes right outside. I tried to close my eyes. Whatever it was, I didn't want to see it.

When I woke, blue had just started to creep into the eastern sky.

I went down for a drink of water and found Ed Wharton sitting at the kitchen table eating toast. Low music came from the radio, something jazzy and slow. Mr. Wharton reached over and turned it off.

"Couldn't sleep?" he said. "Toast?"

"Bad dream," I told him, filling a glass from the tap. "No, thanks."

I sat down at the table in front of him, sipping water while he crunched his crusts. I was sore and tired and thirsty and wished I was asleep.

"It'll be OK, Neil," he said. "You'll see."

"Easy for you to say."

"Is it? My mistake. You're doomed, then. That better?"

"It's honest, at least."

"No, it isn't. It's giving up to think like that. Hope for the best, prepare for the worst. That's the golden rule."

"No it isn't."

"It's one of them. Or it should be. It's one of mine, anyway. Along with keep the diesel topped up, and walk your dragon at least once a day or he'll burn down your whole rig, truck, trailer and all."

"You have a dragon?"

"What? Me? No. No one has a dragon, Neil, and anyone who thinks they do is just a dragon's dinner waiting to happen."

"But you said—"

"Well, it's more that I gave a dragon a lift one time. Picked him up in Scotland. He'd hatched from an egg in someone's kitchen, just an ordinary egg they'd bought with five others from the supermarket, and the children wanted to keep it and the parents wanted to flush it down the toilet. I offered to take it off their hands before something unpleasant happened. Drove it all the way to China. Have you ever tried to drive a truck into China unseen? With a dragon on board? Can't exactly declare it at customs, can you? By the time I got there it was nearly bigger than the truck and eating three or four sheep every night. It was like having a hungry jet fighter in the back. It took off into the mountains without even a backward glance. Still, all for the best."

I laughed.

"That didn't really happen, did it?"

"I can show you the claw marks and the scorching in the trailer, if you like." He raised his eyebrows and looked at me curiously. "Why wouldn't you believe me? You've lived with the Seasons passing through your phone box four times a year for your whole life."

I shifted in my seat.

"Well, yeah, but that's different."

He smiled.

"You're used to it, aren't you? It doesn't seem like magic because something that's been part of your whole life can't really be magic; it's just the way things are. I've met lots of magicians: witches, wizards, druids, sorcerers, conjurers. Most of them live quiet, dull, normal lives, forgetting that the magic they have is, well, magic. To them it's normal. To me it's . . ."

"Stupendous," I said, smiling.

"Exactly." He breathed. "I once wished to have magic, so I went looking for it. And I found it. I found it in all sorts of places. Wherever I found it, I found wonder and excitement and strangeness. But to the people who had the magic, or who watched over it, it was just . . . normal. 'OK,' they'd say with a shrug. 'Have a look. Give it a go. Touch it if you dare.' They couldn't see why I was so interested. They didn't understand what I got out of it. So, in the end, I prefer to be the Tourist. The Tourist finds the magic in the things everyone else has forgot about or thinks are normal. The Tourist finds things amazing and exciting, and maybe he can remind people how amazing and exciting and magic things can be. I don't want to be a magician anymore, Neil. I find magic everywhere I go."

I didn't speak for a while, and we sat there in silence together.

"Looking forward to tomorrow?" Ed asked after a while.

"Yeah," I said with a laugh. "Hey, you mean today! It'll be dawn soon! Everyone's going to be up and—Ow!"

I put my hands to my ears. My eardrums felt as though they had been stabbed through with white-hot needles. Ed's face was twisted with pain.

"It's the pressure!" His voice sounded far, far away, many miles underground. "Like in a plane! Air pressure!"

I doubled over, whimpering. Ed was holding his nose and inflating his cheeks.

Then every window in the house exploded.

CHAPTER 8

LIZ

Everything crashed and broke like a great glasshouse falling apart, with me inside lying on the ground and all the broken glass falling down on me, shiny and sharp and cutting. I woke up with a scream stuck in my throat.

"Hello, Liz," said Mrs. Fitzgerald.

I sat up too fast, making myself gasp for breath, and then I froze. The last thing I could remember was leaning on Dad while climbing the stairs to bed. Now something was howling somewhere nearby. My room was dim and gray and full of moving shadows. The curtains lifted as a breeze blew in through the broken window. There was glass all over the floor. It was almost dawn. Over the howling, I could hear music playing from the alarm clock radio in

Mum and Dad's room. We should be getting up and going downstairs and waiting for the phone to ring.

She was sitting on the end of my bed, and she was smiling and her teeth were sharp and her eyes were green and glowing.

I opened my mouth, but I couldn't speak.

"Good morning, Liz."

Just like that. "Good morning, Liz," she said, uninvited, unwelcome, with monsters screaming and glass broken all around us.

"I wanted to have a quiet word with you before the sun came up. Things are going to get a little unpleasant, Liz. I want you to know that when this is over, I will forgive you for being my enemy. You can come to me whenever you're ready, and I will teach you everything I know. You can come with me now, and save your family a great deal of pain. Do you understand what I'm telling you?"

She was smiling. I'd never seen her smile at anyone else. That made me even more scared. Now she was sitting in the dark at the end of my bed, waiting patiently for me to answer. She'd forgive me? What had I ever done to her? If anyone should be asking for forgiveness it should be her, and it'd be a cold day in hell before she'd get it from me.

Teach me? To be like her? Who could possibly want to be like her?

Way down deep in my soul, in a place where I looked

at her and saw someone tall and scary and beautiful, and then looked at myself and saw someone small and weak and silly, a tiny little voice whispered. *Me*, it said. *I'd like to be like her.*

"Well, Liz?" she demanded.

I could hear a howling and a knocking, things falling and breaking, shouting and crying, like a war going on downstairs. I threw back the covers and leaped from the bed. She put her hand out, palm forward. Her fingers were long and elegant and graceful. There was a twist of annoyance to her smile. I stopped.

"That's Hugh," she said. "Dear sweet Hugh can't help himself. But this is between you and me, Liz. Let the boys have their fun."

I looked at the door, in agony. I could hear the sounds of a high wind blowing, things breaking and smashing, Neil's voice yelling, Mum and Dad and Owen rushing out of their rooms and running for the stairs. I wanted to be with them.

"Stay a moment," she said, and gestured at the bed. I slowly sat down on the edge of the mattress, ready to run for the door, knowing I wouldn't dare. She moved, her dress whispering, her skin glowing, and she was beside me, her hand on mine.

"Poor Liz," she said. "They don't know who you are, do they? The little girl? The mad one, the awkward one, always making trouble, an embarrassment and a shame. They only let you do what you want because it's too much trouble to make you stop."

I tried to pull my hand away. I couldn't move. The cacophony below was getting louder, more frantic and violent. If anyone got hurt . . .

I made to stand up. Her hand gripped my wrist. She rose and brought me with her. Somehow my bare feet passed over the glass on the floor without touching any. Her smile was still gentle, understanding. We swept toward the bedroom window. It gaped like a mouth full of broken teeth. She stooped and swept through and dragged me along behind.

We fell, we flew, sweeping down to land on the lawn in front of the house. Her hand was still around my wrist. My legs shook and my breath came in gasps. Inside the house the sound of the high wind and things breaking and people yelling came through the broken windows. Everything was dark and swirling and confused.

"You could do that," she said. "You could do this, and you could do that. But not with them. With me. I would like a hostage, Liz. I would like an apprentice. I would like a daughter."

The sky was bright. I could see the Weatherbox over the wall at the end of the front lawn. *TELEFÓN*. It was light enough to read and getting lighter by the minute.

Numbly, my ears ringing, a cold sweat making my body shiver, I shook my head. No, no, no, no, please, no.

But part of me, the part that was jealous because I could never become Weatherman, the part that looked at Mrs. Fitzgerald and saw someone strong and powerful and independent, the part that knew that even though we thought she was terrible, she must surely be the hero of her own story, that part, deep down, said yes.

CHAPTER 9

NEIL

The shock of the noise drove me sideways, sliding along the table and tumbling to the floor. I hunched up, bracing myself, as wind rushed in through the windows. Doors blew open and slammed against walls. Things were falling and breaking all around me. The table tilted over onto its side. Ed Wharton tugged and pulled at it until it was facing the wind, and we hid behind it while crockery and cutlery and pots and pans and the blender and the tea towels and the potted plants flew around the room.

Roaring and whistling through every gap and over every surface, the wind, like a riot of invisible serpents, flattened and squeezed and smashed everything it met. Ed and I leaned our weights on the legs of the table, trying to keep it into the wind. It kept trying to tip over and fly away and take us with it.

At least the pain in my ears had gone. I couldn't have stood much more of that.

The fridge was blown across the floor, rocking along until it reached the limit of its electric cable. It was right in front of our table when it began to lean forward, hanging over us, until the weight of it dragged the plug from the wall. We went scrambling away across the floor just as the great ton of metal came crashing down on the table, crushing it to splinters. We went tumbling through the doorway and down the corridor, batted and bashed by flying things that had once been ordinary everyday household objects but were now lethal speeding chunks of pain.

We were on our backs, the force of the wind sucking us toward the living room. The whirlwind filled it. We grabbed hold of the frame of the doorway, our legs stretching as we were pulled toward the center of the thing. I saw the television fly past, the coffee table, Mum's favorite china figurines in jigsaw pieces.

"I can't hold on!" I yelled.

"Me neither!" cried Ed.

Then the cat came in through the broken window, flowing like oily orange smoke, claws unsheathed, teeth bared, bigger than I'd ever seen him. Bigger than any living cat, bigger than a car, big as some mythical prehistoric cat that used to hunt dinosaurs as though they were mice. He pounced at the whirlwind. Flying furniture bounced off him unnoticed. The whirlwind tried to run away.

The wind stopped, and we fell in a heap. The whirlwind bent away from the cat, hurling itself back across the room and against the far wall. The cat crouched, lashed it with its paw, hissed and leaped right into the roaring heart of the thing. Crashing and wailing and yowling, the fighting mass of wind and cat tore around the living room, reducing the already battered furniture to splinters, ripping the carpet from the floor and the paper from the wall. Ed and I scooted back from the doorway, hands held before our faces, as a seething wall of glass and wood and metal scoured through the air in front of us.

I saw the door into the front hall open a crack and a small, frightened face peek through.

"Owen!" I screamed, waving frantically. "Go back! Go back upstairs! Go!"

Owen was pulled away, and Dad's face appeared. Then he jerked back and the door shut once more.

The whirlwind stopped whirling. Two bodies flew in opposite directions, hit opposite walls, and fell to the floor. The cat wailed, bleeding from a hundred cuts. The boy screeched with fear and outrage, jumped to his feet, slipped on the wreckage, but, instead of falling, floated, turning in midair, his face a mask of rage and pain. Hugh Fitzgerald, flying in a limping sort of a way, floated out the window. Neetch, having shrunk back to normal cat size, made one last heroic leap and landed on the small of Hugh's back, and they both disappeared out into the dawn, wailing and screaming like a pair of hell's own choirboys.

CHAPTER 10

LIZ

Mrs. Fitzgerald's smile grew wider, her grip tightened, and she began to turn away from the house, bringing me with her. Out through the living room window came Hugh, screeching and struggling with Neetch, who had dug his claws into Hugh's back. Hugh turned as he flew, went low, and scraped across the lawn, knocking Neetch off. Then Hugh hit the ground and rolled head over heels to a groaning stop at his mother's feet.

She looked at me, her smile gone, then down at Hugh.

Neetch stalked across the grass, growing, blocking out the house, dwarfing us, mouth wide, teeth like sharp white fence posts, tongue red as blood. Mrs. Fitzgerald let go of my wrist and with both hands drew in the air a strange design that burned with green flame and fell like a net over Neetch's face and head. The cat howled and shrank, and suddenly the air was full of the smell of burned fur and skin. I jumped over Hugh's prone body and gathered Neetch up in my hands. He was no bigger than a kitten, mewling pitifully, fur smoking.

I backed away from her, and she watched me go, saying nothing. She stooped and helped Hugh upright. Over at the gate, John-Joe stood with his feet spread and his shotgun ready.

"Is he OK? Is he OK? Is he OK?" Owen cried as he ran up, reaching for Neetch, and I gave him over as gently as I could, then pushed them behind me and kept backing toward the house. Mum, Dad, and Neil rushed out and stopped beside me. Mum put her hand on my shoulder, and Dad stepped toward Mrs. Fitzgerald and Hugh. His face was flushed and red and his teeth were bared and he was breathing in through his mouth and I could see his chest rise and fall. I had never seen Dad so angry.

"You have committed more crimes today than I can count. You have broken rules and violated agreements laid down so long ago there was barely language to express them. You will pay us back for everything your son has damaged or destroyed and if I see him near my children or near my house ever again as long as he lives, I will make sure he regrets it. You will answer for your grotesque and insane interference with the weather and the Seasons and with me! Now, get out of here, get off my lawn and off my road and do not come back."

Mrs. Fitzgerald looked at Dad as if she'd never seen him before, as if she were noticing him for the first time. She tilted her head slightly to one side. I thought I could see tiny lights flickering in the backs of her shadowy eyes, way, way down, like bombs going off in a faraway place.

Neil ran across the lawn toward the gate. Hugh made to block him, but his mother touched his arm and he stopped with a groan of pain. *Good,* I thought. Fitzy shook his shotgun, but didn't point it, and Neil jumped over the wall and stood beside the phone box and looked back.

"Dad!" he said. "Come on!"

The sun was coming up. The sun was coming up way over in the east, down at the end of the road, bright and rosy. Dew had fallen and everything was wet and shining. My feet were bare and numb, and I shivered with the cold and with the knowing. The light reached the Weather-box. We held our breaths, and waited. The phone did not ring.

"DAD!" yelled Neil.

"Is something wrong?" said Mrs. Fitzgerald. Dad glared.

"Get away from here, I said!" Dad was yelling now. "Go on!"

"Or what? What could you do to me? Where are your

vassals and retainers, oh King of the Four Quarters? Where are your wise men of power and your warriors bold? Hollow King of an Empty Quarter, I name you. I scorned worse than you from the pillows of my crib, and that was long, long ago, when there was real power in the world."

Ed Wharton loomed up beside me, like a friendly rolling boulder. The sun was halfway clear of the horizon now. Neil was staring down the road at it, his hand held before his face to shield his eyes.

"I think you'd better leave," Ed rumbled. "You're not welcome here. You've done enough damage."

"But I haven't finished," she said. "I have come here to issue a challenge to the Weatherman. I challenge you, Weatherman. I say you are unfit for your task. I say you have failed in your duties as your father failed before you. I challenge you, Weatherman. I say you are incompetent and careless and irresponsible, as your father was before you. I say the Seasons are not safe in your hands. I say it is time you were deposed and another put in your place. Someone fit for the task. I challenge you, Weatherman. *I have said it three times.* You will be cast off, and I will take your place."

Dad stared, still breathing hard. Ed Wharton was holding him back; otherwise I think he might have run at her.

"You can't challenge me. You can't cast me off. You can't take my place. It can't be done."

"Can't it? The Weatherman has been cast off and re-placed before."

"Once," Dad said. "But that was—"

"Listen," she said, tilting her head to one side. "The morning sun has grown full and bright. Where is the bell? Why does nothing ring? Where is the Autumn, Weather-man? Look to your task. You are failing."

Ed Wharton's eyes grew wide, and his hands dropped from Dad's arm.

"You, you can't," Dad stammered. "Nobody could . . ." Dad took a step toward her, his hand in a fist. "What have you done? Dear God, what the hell have you done?"

"What have *you* done, Weatherman? Why does the Sum-mer linger? If the Weatherman does not know, then who does? Who does the Weatherman answer to? How long do you think it will take before they grow tired of your failure? A day? Two? They will grow restless and angry, Weatherman, and then they will come, and you will answer for yourself. They will find you wanting, and I will be there to take your place."

And then Dad grew, and changed, and for a moment he wasn't Dad but something huge and green and earthy and alive. Mrs. Fitzgerald's face was eager.

"That's it, Weatherman. Unleash your power. Set the seal on your failure. Only a coward and a weakling would stand before a mortal enemy who would take from him everything he possessed, strip him to the bone of all he loved and leave that enemy alive and whole to do their worst when he has the means to scour her from the earth."

Dad was doing that one thing a Weatherman is utterly forbidden from doing. He was becoming Summer right before our very eyes. I could feel the heat radiating off him. He was going to roast her to a crisp and scatter her ashes with a south wind and when he was done the Seasons would come and throw him off the planet.

"That's enough."

Mum suddenly stood between Dad and Mrs. Fitzgerald, and the heat faded and Dad was Dad again, small and human and struggling for control.

"I know you," Mum said. She was a head shorter than either Dad or Mrs. Fitzgerald and wearing a worn dressing gown and fluffy slippers, but her voice was level and cool.

"I know your sort and I know your make and I know your mark. By the cow in the barn and the goat in the pen and the oak in the grove, I say you, be away before the sun rises no more than the length of my fingernail or the black waters can have you and the rushes fill your hair."

Without another word, Mrs. Fitzgerald swept away to the gate, dragging Hugh with her, and she and her husband and her son crossed the road and vanished into the trees. We rushed to the phone box. Neil was still staring at the sun. Dad had both hands in his hair. Owen cradled Neetch. Mum looked like thunder, and Ed Wharton just looked sad and bewildered and scared.

I put my head back and screamed my rage at the sky.

A phone rang, but it was the phone in the house. No one moved to go in and answer it. It stopped, and then started ringing again.

The Weatherbox was silent.

PART 2

The Maloneys and the Hags of the Black Pool

CHAPTER 11

NEIL

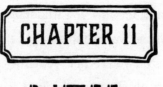

It was an hour later and Liz was still making a flipping eejit out of herself.

"Twiggy man, bring the cold. Twiggy man, bring the cold."

"God, Liz, shut UP!"

She ignored me and kept dancing and chanting.

"Twiggy man, bring the cold! Twiggy man, bring the cold!"

At least she wasn't screaming at the sky anymore.

Mum and Dad were sitting side by side on the wall, heads close together, talking in low voices. Now that Mum had Dad calmed down a bit, I could barely hear what they were saying, even though I was sitting beside Dad. Ed sat beside Mum. Owen had taken poor hurt Neetch inside to put cream on his sore bits. And Liz kept embarrassing us all with her stupid antics. On today of all days—the most horrible day ever.

Can you imagine? Can you understand how huge this was? It was as if the world had stopped turning. If you stop a car suddenly and you're not wearing your seat belt you get thrown through the windshield. I looked up and wondered if we were all going to get thrown through the sky and off the planet. People, animals, trees, cities, mountains, seas, all pitched into space because Mrs. Fitzgerald had put her foot on the brake.

And yet nothing happened. Nothing changed. Today was the same as yesterday. Of course it was. Yesterday was Summer, and so was today. But that was the problem. Things can't stay the same in this world. Things change or things die. Things come to an end.

Mum was disagreeing with Dad about something. Dad was shaking his head and saying he had no choice. His hair was a mess and his eyes moved around like they were trying to see everything at once, or avoid seeing it. He looked wild.

"I have to stay," he said, getting loud again. "I have to stay here. It's stupid, but there's nothing else I can do. If I leave, it's . . . dereliction. I would be deserting my post. If I do that, I won't deserve to be Weatherman."

I thought of derelict houses with crumbling walls and

broken windows all covered in ivy, and I thought of the Weatherbox with all its glass shattered and the wood rotten and eaten and the phone pulled off and the door hanging open. I filled up with panic and fear and a kind of hurt that made me want to scream out how horrible and unfair this was.

"Then I'll go," Mum said. "I'll do it."

"I wish you could. But if it can't be me, then it has to be Neil in my place, speaking with my voice."

"What?" I said. "Me? What?"

"Then I'll take him!" Mum said, louder. "I'll go with him!"

"No! I'm sorry, but just look at what's happened! The danger is here! Mrs. Fitzgerald is incredibly dangerous. I can't even conceive of how she managed to stop the Seasons. And she tried to take Liz! Hugh has completely wrecked the house—it's a miracle nobody was hurt. No. Owen and Liz need us both, here, protecting them. Besides, Neil won't be going alone."

"Going where?" I asked.

Dad looked at Mum, and then looked at me.

"You're going to find the Shieldsmen," he said.

"I am?"

"You are."

"He is?" Liz said. At last she stopped chanting and dancing. Her face was pale. "No," she said. "Not that.

93

That's mine. *I'm* the Shieldsman. *He's* the Weatherman. He can't have both!"

"Liz," Dad said. "Listen—"

"That's not right! That's not fair! I'll go! I'll find them! I'll bring them back! I will!"

"No, Liz, you can't," Dad said. "They answer only to the Weatherman. Or his heir."

"Him, you mean," she said, pointing at me. "Him. Not me."

"Liz—" I began.

"Shut up," she said, jumped the wall, and ran back to the house.

"Well," Mum said, "that's done it."

"What's wrong with her?" I asked. "What did I do?"

"You were born first," Mum said. "You were born a boy. And the chain of succession for the Weathermen was established by a bunch of Stone Age men."

I swallowed and nodded. Today was a day for ruining things. Today was a day for everything to be spoiled and wrecked and made horrible.

"Now, your Dad and I are asking Mr. Wharton to drive *you* to Dublin, instead of your Dad. That's a big responsibility, so he might say no. If he says yes, then you will go to the Weathermen's Club—we have a key if there's no one there to let you in. Look around and see if you can find a clue or a way to contact the Shieldsmen."

"There's not much chance," Dad said. "There's probably nothing there, so you need only be away for a few hours. If you find anything, call me. If it looks like there's a real chance of finding them, then I'll go to them and bring them back myself."

"Is that OK with you, Mr. Wharton?" Mum asked.

Mr. Wharton shifted, rocking slightly from side to side on the wall.

"Sure. It'll be fun."

"But Dad," I said, "what are you going to do about the Autumn? What are you going to do about *her*?"

Dad winced.

"I don't know, Neil. I'll sit here and wait for the phone to ring—nobody else can answer it. I need to find out why it's not ringing. My God! How do you block a Season? You don't! I need to work out what she's done. And then, to take action, I'll need reinforcements. I'll need the club and I'll need the Shieldsmen and I don't think we have much time."

"Right," Mum said. "You'd better get going then. The sooner you go, the sooner you'll be back. Oh God, is that the house phone again?"

We went inside, stepping carefully around broken glass and crockery. The phone had stopped ringing again by the time we got there. Mum stood in the living room, surveyed the damage, and lit a cigarette. Dad touched her elbow, then stole her cigarette and took a quick puff. Liz glared at everybody and kicked something broken across the floor, breaking it some more.

I went upstairs and got dressed, and then they all walked us down to the old barn where Ed had parked his truck and waved us off without much ceremony. Mum gave me a squeeze, Dad clapped me on the shoulder, Liz gave me a long hard stare, and Owen was too preoccupied with Neetch to do anything other than give me a wide-eyed look from between a pair of twitching, furry, triangular cat ears.

Mum turned to Ed. "You keep him safe and sound, you understand? Back by dinner. No sightseeing. No trouble."

Dad shook Ed's hand.

"What she said," he said.

Ed grinned. "All aboard!" he yelled, and climbed nimbly up through the door.

The cab of Ed's truck was clean and tidy and smelled of air freshener and leather furniture polish. There was no rubbish or dust on the dashboard, no tacky souvenirs or rude pictures or stickers with hilarious jokes. It was spotless.

Ed put both hands on the wheel and looked at the road with wistful eyes.

Then he roared, and the engine roared with him, and we left home and made our way out into the world.

CHAPTER 12

LIZ

Neil went off with Ed in Ed's big truck to have adventures and do cool things while we stayed behind to work and work and work. I was mad, but I was sorry I'd said what I'd said. Those things were my secret and saying them out loud only hurt everyone and showed what a silly little girl I was. I tried to be a little more like normal, even though nothing would be normal ever again. I tried to give Mum and Dad a way to think that everything was OK.

"Stupid Neil," I said. "Why does he get to go?"

"He's got a job to do," Dad said. "And so do we, OK? We have to guard the phone box and the house and protect each other."

"They'll get into trouble," I warned. "Neil always gets into trouble."

"So do you," said Owen. Tiny Neetch purred in the crook of his arm. "You get into trouble all the time."

"Yeah, but when I get into trouble, it's other people who have the trouble and not me. Neil's just a trouble *magnet*. I'm more of a trouble*maker*."

"Yes, we know," said Mum, and she tried to give a bright, encouraging smile, though it came across as more of a hideous snarl. "Now, let's all go decide whether it'd be easier to start tidying the house or to just burn it down and build another one."

Really? That's what we were going to do instead of stopping Mrs. Fitzgerald?

Everything was broken, everything was torn, everything was wet and stained and smelly. It was almost interesting how Hugh had done all of this, just him. He had broken Mum's favorite porcelain statue and destroyed all the framed photographs of us and the paintings Mum's mum had done of the sea and the mountains and the birds. The stuffing from the sofa and the armchairs was spread all over the walls and the ceiling. One half of the broken coffee table was embedded in the plaster of the wall. The chairs had lost all their legs.

He had done all of this, and in a way that was kind of amazing and cool, even though it made me angry and plot revenge.

"Hugh, you do, then we do you," I chanted.

If he could do this, what could *she* do? I wondered.

I didn't make a chant for *her*. I didn't dare.

The kitchen was even worse, and all that mess was in the way of our breakfast, so we started there until we had cleared enough to let Mum start cooking. Owen and I went to sit on the stairs and mope and smell breakfast.

Dad was sitting on the floor of the living room, cross-legged, eyes shut tight. The phone was beside him, balanced on a pile of broken stuff that had been our sofa. He was watching out for more atmospheric attacks on the house, and taking a break every now and then to try calling the Weathermen's Club. They still weren't answering.

There was a knock on the door. We stepped over the piles of broken stuff and opened it.

Standing on the step outside were Ed Wharton's hags— tall, thin, crooked old women, leaning on tall, thin, crooked old sticks. Their long white hair hung down to their waists in huge frizzy knots, full of leaves and twigs and cobwebs and spiders. Their faces were covered in wrinkles, their mouths had no teeth, their clothes were muddy and torn, and they had no shoes or socks on their feet.

I swung the door shut. Too late. One of them hit the door with the end of her stick and pushed it back against me. She was stronger than she looked.

"Hello!" the other one said, coming inside, leaning over us. "We'd like a room!"

"With a bed!" said the first old woman, stepping inside too and making a muddy footprint on the floor.

"Two beds!"

"And a working toilet!"

"And one of those things where the water all comes out and it's like you're in the rain only the water is all lovely and warm!"

"Two of those as well, please!"

"And breakfasts!"

"Two breakfasts!"

"In bed! With hot tea in cups!"

"In the warm rain thing!"

"Don't be silly! Your tea would get wet!"

I pulled Owen behind me and backed away from the doorway. One of the old women stiffened and peered sharply down at Owen.

"What is that?"

"What is what?" said the other.

"The boy."

"The boy? It's a boy? Shocking!"

"The boy. The boy has a cat."

"So? Boys have cats. Give a boy a cat and he has a friend for life. A boy and his cat off on their merry adventures."

"*Our* cat!"

"*Our* cat? Unpossible!"

"Calamity! Treachery!"

"Catnapper! Bad boy! Bad cat!"

"Go away!" I said, moving backward, pushing Owen along behind me. The two old women followed us down the hallway, their sticks raised, pointing, their hair alive, wriggling with spiders, fluttering with moths, buzzing with flies, their eyes dark and malicious. Neetch struggled in Owen's arms, yowling.

"Not without our cat!"

"Not without our breakfast!"

"We'll have cat for breakfast!"

"Useless cat!"

"Tasty cat!"

"Tasty boy!"

"Oh, no, dear. Cat for breakfast."

"Boy for lunch?"

"Lovely!"

"Hello?" said Dad coming into the hall with Mum. "Can I help?"

Me and Owen ran and hid behind them.

"They want to eat us!" wailed Owen.

"Don't be silly!" said one of the women in a tiny, creaky voice like a door blown open by a breeze. They were suddenly bent and stooped and leaning on their sticks again, looking old and fragile and weird but not scary.

"We want beds!"

"And breakfasts!"

"We have moneys!"

"Lots of moneys!"

They reached into hidden pockets and threw torn and crumpled and dirty notes on the floor, along with a few wood lice and a bright red centipede.

"So much moneys!"

"We have been saving all our moneys for years and years, and all so we can have a lovely holiday in your beautiful house of beds and breakfasts!"

"And warm rain!"

"And sweet, sweet children!"

"So delicious!"

"And well behaved!"

Neetch was complaining loudly and furiously trying to swipe at the old women with his claws.

"Take him outside," Mum said, and Owen fled, but I stayed.

While Dad took a dustpan and brush to the insects, Mum picked up the money, straightened it, scraped some of the dirt off it, taped some of it together, found an envelope, stuck the money in the envelope, and put the envelope in her back pocket. Then she showed the ladies the guestbook and asked them to sign in. The old ladies spat on their hands, then spat on the tip of the pen and each drew a strange scrawl, spirals and lines and squiggles, instead of names.

Their signs reminded me of something, something bright and hot in the darkness.

Mum studied them for a moment. Her lips were thin and her face was pale and her hands shook slightly. Maybe she was thinking about what she'd said last night—about the hags helping us against Mrs. Fitzgerald. Perhaps just saying it the way she had had been a kind of invitation to them, or maybe they would have come anyway. I don't know if she and Dad could have made them go away, so maybe the best thing to do was to make them welcome and hope they were more or less on our side.

Mum shut the book, smiled her most welcoming woman-of-the-house smile, and led them to their room. I followed, keeping well out of reach of their sticks. Mum apologized for the state of the place, all the broken windows and furniture and stuff.

"Oh, my dear," one of them said. "I hope you didn't go to all that trouble just for us! How sweet!"

"Just like home!" the other said. "I hope you have chorizo! We do like chorizo! Perhaps a snack of chorizo and a nice cup of tea for dipping? That would be nice!"

They squealed with delight when Mum showed them into the room, and one began jumping up and down on the bed and the other went straight to the shower and turned it on and climbed in fully dressed. The wildlife in her hair was soon going to be clogging up our drains.

Mum told them the time for breakfast, and then we fled.

"Mum," I said. "Should we really have them in the house? They're dangerous. They're her sisters!"

"I don't think we could have kept them out, hon. It's hard to say no to that sort of . . . person when they call around. We'll just have to hope they don't mean to harm us, and that when push comes to shove they'll want to put her back in her shell. I mean, what's the worst that could happen?"

"They could kiss and make up and decide to help her be Weatherman?"

"Yes," Mum said. "That *would* be about the worst. Still, we're OK until breakfast. Hospitality and kind treatment can go a long way with people like them, as Mr. Wharton has shown. I'm hoping they'll really like the shower."

"The spiders probably won't."

"The what?"

"Never mind, Mum."

———◦•◦———

The dining room had, thank the Lord, not been touched by Hugh's rampage, so we sat at a table and devoured our own breakfast and then the hags came sweeping in calling for food and tea and newspapers. They seemed different—less haglike, taller and straighter than they had been before. They weren't wearing their old raggy rags anymore, either. They had long loose dresses on now, all white and shiny, and their eyes didn't seem as dark and their faces didn't seem as wrinkled. They smiled pleasantly and seemed to have somehow grown a few teeth. Weirdest of all, their hair seemed shorter and less silvery.

"It's miraculous," one said, sitting on her chair and putting a napkin across her lap. "Positively miraculous what a nice hot stream of clean water will do for you. Isn't it, my dear?"

"To be sure, my dear," said the other. "Much better than simply rolling in the furze bushes once a year whether you need to or not. I feel like a new person!"

"Speaking of new persons, I could eat one for breakfast!"

"Oh, my darling, no need! Look at the delicacies promised by this menu! Muesli! I rather fancy some muesli! I do like foreign food! I hope it's not too spicy!"

"Oh, go on, you, you always had a taste for the exotic! I myself will dine on cuts of slaughtered pig, blood pudding, and chicken embryos. I may even ask for two chicken embryos!"

"Um, uh, how do you want them cooked?" I asked, trying to take all this down on the notebook. "The, uh, embryos and stuff, I mean."

"Cooked?" said the lady. "Oh, well, why not? Yes, go on then, cook them."

"Right," I said, and fled to the kitchen, where Mum and Dad were heating the frying pan and boiling the kettle. Owen was hiding behind the fridge.

"Stay away from them," I whispered to him, and Dad broke a few eggs into the hot frying pan.

When I brought in their breakfasts, they were reading newspapers. I had no idea where the newspapers had come from.

"Such strange goings-on in the world," one remarked.

"Indeed, my dear. We aren't safe in our beds."

"Or our showers."

"Did you see this? An indoor flood!"

"Oh my goodness, how dreadful! Did they have too many showers?"

"No idea, my dear, but it sounds terribly dangerous, what with wind and rain all over the place!"

"What fun!"

"No, dear, how awful!"

"I do beg your pardon. How awfully fun. How terribly, terribly fun!"

"I see by your paper that there was a kidnapping!"

"There was?"

"Yes, dear, there was. It says so. On your paper."

"Does it? Oh, my dear, I forgot how to read years ago. I was just looking at the pictures."

"Bizarre, bizarre trouble, dear."

"How dreadful! Dreadfully, dreadfully fun!"

"Those are last weeks' newspapers," I said, looking at the dates. They glanced at me and smiled.

"Clever child!"

"How can she tell?"

"The dates, dear."

"Terribly, terribly, deliciously clever!"

"Perhaps she knows all about the big fight?"

"The dreadful, dreadful fight!"

"In the woods with the policemen and the people and the trees."

"Trees fighting people and policemen! What will they think of next?"

The newspaper rustled.

"Oh, blood will flow and heads will roll and limbs will be chopped off! If only they could fly!"

"What are they teaching in the schools these days? Imagine not being able to fly!"

I backed away from the table, keeping them in sight until I was out of the room. They smiled and waved at me the whole time.

CHAPTER 13

NEIL

Ed Wharton drove, and I sat and enjoyed the view over the hedges and through the trees. I loved to see the spread of fields and the wrinkling hills and the huddled woods and copses. Cattle grazed and horses trotted amiably through meadows seeded with wildflowers and tall, protective grasses. Purple mountains shouldered their way across the horizon like disgruntled giants, and the sun shone warmly through the yellow sky and the massive windshield, heating the plastic molding on the dashboard. After about half an hour, the heat and the sickly sky and the motion of the hedges and houses and electricity poles as they went past on either side began to make me feel ill. I sank back in my seat and groaned.

I looked over at Ed Wharton. I would be lying if I said I was happy about being sent off to Dublin with a more or less complete stranger for company while the Fitzgeralds were threatening my family, but I told myself it was OK. It'd be a quick trip. There and back.

"Are we nearly there yet?"

Ed Wharton sighed and smiled.

"Soon," he said.

"Soon we'll be there, or soon we'll be nearly there?" I asked.

"Yes," he said.

"Right," I said.

The cab shuddered as he downshifted roughly and took us around a sharp corner.

"Hey, easy there," I said. "It's not a race car, you know."

"Yes it is."

"It's a great big truck. Race cars are smaller and faster and they look like the letter T with wheels."

"It's not a race car, but it *is* a racing truck. It's a truck, and I raced it in a race. In a race it doesn't matter what you are, all that matters is who gets over the finishing line first."

"Oh. Did you win?"

"Heh. God, no."

"Did you come second?"

"Not even close."

"Did you lose? Did you come last?"

"I certainly did."

"You seem awfully happy about it. What was this race?"

"Have you ever heard of the Island of Abasa?"

"No."

"It's a little rock in the Mediterranean. I mean, literally a rock. It's about two meters wide."

"Yeah?"

"We had to race across it. Took us four days."

"That's a long time to go two meters."

"That's because they shrunk us down to the size of ants."

"Who did?"

"The Wives of Abasa. There were four of them and they were looking for husbands."

"I'm pretty sure it wouldn't take an ant four days to cover two meters."

"It would if they were desperately trying to lose the race."

"Why did you want to lose the race?" I asked. "Oh. Because the winners got to be the husbands to the Wives of Abasa, right?"

Ed nodded. "Right."

"No, wait, if they were wives, wouldn't they already have husbands?"

"Technically they were widows."

"And the old husbands?"

"Funny story, that. The Wives of Abasa are beautiful marble statues, and they live in a beautiful but ancient stone temple in the waters just off the island. One of the temple pillars fell on the four husbands and crushed them to pieces."

"That's not funny."

"No? You should have seen the expression on their faces. Anyway, the four wives needed four new husbands, so they held a race for the honor of their cold white hands."

"If you didn't want to marry one of them, why did you enter the race?"

"Another funny story. I was just driving through Greece, minding my own business, when suddenly this chariot pulls out in front of me."

"Chariot?"

"Yup. Horses, reins, rider, whip, the whole kit and caboodle. Dressed up in old-style armor the charioteer was, riding hell for leather, pursued by a giant marble ox. Anyway, I veered off the road to avoid hitting the chariot, straight into the charging marble ox who scooped me up in his horns and carried me off to the Isle of Abasa, where I was shrunk to the size of an ant and made to race against four other guys in chariots."

"So you were in a truck and they were just in chariots, and you still lost?"

"Wasn't easy."

"Didn't you want to be married to a beautiful marble statue?"

"Wouldn't have lasted. We'd nothing in common."

For a while we drove on in silence. I didn't mean to drift off, but I did, and slept most of the way into Dublin. I was gently prodded into wakefulness by the voices on Ed's radio talking about weird atmospheric phenomena and strange behavior reported by pet owners. Dogs had stopped barking. Cats had stopped purring. Budgies had stopped singing. Fish had stopped swimming. And turtles refused to come out of their shells. It sounded like a silly season story, the announcer said, until you realized that it wasn't just a few cranks; it was hundreds of cranks, all saying the same thing.

"It's as if the animals are worrying about something," one of the guests remarked.

"Must be the economy," someone said, and everyone laughed.

"Maybe it's the weather!" suggested the announcer. Nobody laughed.

"Maybe it is," someone said. "Have you looked out a window lately? Have you ever seen the sky that color?"

"Well, that's why we have a meteorologist on the panel!" said the announcer. "So how about it? What on earth is up with the weather, and why is the sky yellow?"

"I have absolutely no idea," replied the meteorologist.

The radio cut out in a haze of static when Ed swerved off the street and down a ramp into an underground garage. It was empty, except for Ed's truck, and dark, except for Ed's torch and an exit light over the door at the far end.

"Right," Ed said, when we were out on the street. "Let's see if I can remember how to get there from here."

We found the Weathermen's Club on a quiet, Georgian street a short walk from the center of the city. The row of terraced houses was old and dignified and expensive-looking, except the one with the brass plaque beside the door that read *Weathermen's Club* in big curling letters, and underneath, in smaller letters, *Deliveries Around Back*. The brass was weathered and worn and faded and scratched. It had not been polished for a very long time. The windows were all boarded up. So was the door. The wrought-iron gate in front of the steps was rusted, and down in the basement, behind the railing, there were piles of rubbish and leaves.

I had a key. Dad had given it to me and warned me not to lose it. It would grant me access to the venerable halls of the Weathermen's Club, where I would be treated with the deference and respect due to the Weatherman's son and heir. I hadn't lost the key, but I was beginning to think that I should've brought a hammer and crowbar instead.

"I don't think anyone's at home," Ed said.

I stood in front of the door with the key in my hand, waiting for a keyhole to magically appear on the warped wooden board nailed across the door frame. There was some sort of notice glued to it, but it was worn and torn and I couldn't work out what it was trying to tell me. I studied the graffiti for a clue or a message or a map. It was all dates and squiggles and love hearts.

"Here," said Ed, pushing past. "Let me."

He made a fist, raised his arm, and began pounding on the board.

"Hello? Hello? Anyone home? Hello?"

"Ed, stop," I said, though not very loudly. This whole thing was leaving me a bit depressed.

Ed kept pounding. And pounding and pounding and pounding. Most people would have given up after the first minute. Without interrupting the hammering, he turned his head and gave me a wink.

"Stop it, Ed," I said. He stopped.

"Sorry, did you say something?" he asked.

"Stop hitting the door, Ed."

"Oh. Are you sure? I could keep this up all day. When it comes to magical entrances you have to be persistent. Even if you don't know the magic word, they'll usually let you in if you annoy them enough."

"It's not magical, Ed. It's just boarded up."

"Could be a magical board."

"Yeah, right, Ed. Magical board. Hey, board! Open sesame!"

The board slowly tilted forward. We jumped to either

side as it fell onto the steps and slid down to the footpath. Underneath was an old red door, and there was the lock. The key fit and the door opened without any trouble and we went inside.

It was dark, dusty, and cool, and smelled damp and sour and smoky, as if someone had lit a fire not so long ago and burned something nasty. Sunlight slanted in beams through the windows on either side of the door. Sad old shadows rested in every corner. The walls were made of paneled wood and the floor was covered with cheap plastic linoleum that peeled away from the skirting boards. The overhead light fittings had been stripped away and cracks zigzagged along the yellowing plaster in the ceiling.

"Hello?" I called. Nobody answered.

"Come on," said Ed. "Let's explore."

He was already walking off down the hallway, trying doors and rapping his knuckles on the wooden panels. I went after him, rapping on any spots I thought he missed.

There wasn't much to see, unless seeing how empty and deserted and run down the place was counted, which I suppose it did. I'd always got the impression that this was a hushed and hallowed place, full of varnished wood and velvet trimmings and wise old men who smoked cigars and drank brandy and looked up with annoyance whenever anyone breathed too loudly. I'd imagined stiffly upright butlers gliding by as though on well-oiled wheels, fires burning and crackling in the grates all the year round, bookshelves filled with ancient volumes of facts and figures lining every room, portraits of valued members looking fierce and bad-tempered, possibly because they were dead, gracing the walls. Well, this place might have looked like that once. Not anymore. Not for a long time.

All the rooms were empty. All the shelves were bare. The paintings had been taken down from their hooks. The trimmings had been stripped. The butlers had rolled themselves away. The wise old men had been carted off having smoked their last cigar and sniffed their last brandy. The Weathermen's Club was an empty shell. There was nobody here to help anyone.

We went upstairs to find more empty rooms, and upstairs again to even more empty rooms. One thing the Weathermen's Club had plenty of was empty rooms. There were cobwebs in every corner, mouse droppings on every floor, mold on all the windows. The building was slipping bit by bit from being vacant to being derelict. It wasn't spooky. It was depressing. That was almost worse.

There were no Shieldsmen here. No clues, no signs, no secrets, no revelations.

"Come on," I said. "Let's go."

I locked the door and together we lifted the board back over it. We'd no hammer and nails to secure it, so we left it leaning there, waiting for a stiff breeze or a vandal to come along and knock it down again.

"What's that?" said Ed, pointing at the faded notice on the board.

I peered at it.

"It's all smeared and torn. Let me see. There's a squiggle, a dash, a something, another something . . . AtmoLab! What's an AtmoLab?"

"AtmoLab?" said Ed. "What's that short for, Atmospheric Laboratory? Probably a club designed to look like a laboratory with soft lighting and smooth jazz on the sound system. Nice."

"No, no, it's on the notice. *AtmoLab* is the only word I can make out. Is it a clue? Please tell me it's a clue."

"Even if it isn't, it might be a cool place to hang out for the afternoon," Ed said. "Hang on."

He took out an iPhone and began to slide and tap his fingers around the screen. I sat on the step and watched the traffic go by while I waited.

I know I was aware of the birds before I really noticed them. I'd seen them at home, around the house, and along the road all the way up to Dublin, but it was a scary moment when I looked around and finally *really* saw them. Everywhere.

On the houses, they lined the roofs and the gutters,

crowded together in uneven rows. Perched on electricity and telephone wires and street lamps, sitting wing to wing. Every now and then one of them would ruffle its feathers or stretch its beak wide without making a sound. Crows, robins, swallows, thrushes, wrens, martens, wagtails. All of those and hundreds more. Every type and species, all crushed together. Jackdaws beside sparrows beside gulls beside finches.

I shivered, remembering that old horror film Mum had let us stay up late to watch one night. The one with the birds, which should have been completely daft, but wasn't. I could feel thousands of black, beady eyes watching me. I thought about what I'd heard on the radio.

We were all caught in this terrible pause in the turning of the Seasons. People didn't understand it yet, but the birds did. They were waiting for the rhythm to start again, or to change, or to end. Had the worms in the ground stopped wriggling? Had rabbits and badgers and foxes and rats and mice all stopped moving and grazing and hunting and eating?

Sitting on the steps outside the derelict Weathermen's Club, I could feel the edge of a great catastrophe creeping toward me. How long would they survive like this? How long before they all simply dropped dead where they sat or stood or lay? And how long would we survive without them?

Were we all slowly winding down to a final halt, a stillness and a sleepiness that would leave us standing, empty-minded, empty-eyed on roadsides, in doorways and kitchens, sitting in cars, as though we had been moving all our lives to a beat we couldn't hear, and with that beat gone we could move no more?

Or maybe we wouldn't last that long. What were the Seasons doing right now? Waiting patiently for the Doorways to open? Or getting angry because after millennia, the system had finally failed? And if they got angry enough to decide they didn't need Weathermen anymore, what then? Could something as huge as this really start with something as small as our tiny old Weatherbox and a phone that didn't ring?

"According to this," Ed said at last, "AtmoLab Inc. is a company involved in the development of technologies to monitor and control atmospheric conditions for agricultural and maritime purposes. Monitor and control, eh? I like the sound of that."

"Right," I agreed, "So what's their name doing on the board over the door of the club? Hey, maybe it *is* the club! Maybe they, like, rebranded themselves because they wanted to be young and hip and stuff! Do they have an office anywhere?"

Ed sat beside me on the step and showed me the phone.

"This is their website. There's not much on it—just lots of pretty pictures of sunsets and seascapes. But, look, their headquarters is here in Dublin, down by the canal."

I looked at the tiny screen and tried to pretend I didn't have a feeling that we were wasting precious time and that Dad had sent me up here to keep me out of the way, to protect his heir in case anything happened to him. Then I saw the name.

"Oh," I said.

"What?"

"Look. Their CEO."

"Yeah? What about him?"

"I know that name. Do you know how to get there?"

"Of course. It's not far," Ed said, taking the phone back and reading the name. "Huh. Never heard of him."

"Let's go," I said, striding away from the club. "Come on! Hurry!"

"Er, other way, Neil," Ed said. "So how come you're so fired up all of a sudden? Is it the CEO?"

I continued walking in what I now hoped was the right direction.

"Hey, Neil!" Ed called after me. "Come on! Who's this Tony Holland fella?"

CHAPTER 14

LIZ

The house was still horrible, but it was too hot to do any more, and anyway we were too miserable and worried. Dad took a deck chair and put it down right beside the phone box. He sat leaning forward with his elbows on his knees and his fingers all clasped together in front of his mouth, looking at the middle of the road. Owen was on the lawn, hovering over Neetch, watching him anxiously. The hag ladies hid themselves away in their rooms. For a while nothing happened.

There were birds on all the wires and on the roof and in the trees. None of them flew, none of them sang or croaked. They were looking, too.

I made a chant, and I danced around the house singing it.

"Leafyman, leave here,

Birds fly in the air.

Leaves die, fall down

Hedgehog sleeps in the ground!"

My shoelaces were untied and they flew and flapped as I danced, and kitten Neetch jumped and pounced and chased them around my feet.

"Who's the leafy man?" Owen asked as he watched Neetch play with my laces.

"The Season," I said. "The Summer. She's stuck here and she's angry."

"Why is he leafy? Seasons are all air and water and stuff."

"She's been the Summer for thousands and thousands of years, so she looks a bit like the Summer now—or how the Summer would look if it was a thing."

"How do you know?"

"I sometimes see her in my dreams. Far off. The sun is so bright in my eyes, I can barely make her out. I hide, because I don't want her to see me seeing her. I don't think the Seasons like being seen."

"What does he look like?"

"Leafyman," I sang. "Leafyman, Leafyman."

"Why do you keep saying 'her' and 'she' but when you sing you say 'Leafyman'?"

"Because that's the word you use. When you are something you're a something-man. A policeman. A fireman. A

Shieldsman. So everyone thinks you have to be a man to be these things, even though there are women policemen and women firemen and women Shieldsmen. But I think man isn't just man; it's short for *wo*man too, see? So I don't say policewoman or firewoman or Shieldswoman, because that makes you different from all the policemen and fire- men and Shieldsmen and people might say you're not a proper one of them because of the woman bit at the end. So I'm a Shieldsman and the man at the end is just short for woman, and the Summer is Leafyman, but it's a she."

"You should be the Weatherman," Owen said. "Dad says it's going to be Neil, but I think it should be you. I don't think Neil will like being a Weatherman much."

"I can't be the Weatherman. I'm a girl."

I sang and danced some more.

"I'm sorry," Owen said.

I pretended I didn't hear him. I hopped and kicked and Neetch jumped and swiped at my laces with his tiny paws.

Mum came and sat on the doorstep and watched me while she sipped tea from her favorite red mug that I had got her for Christmas one year. I stopped dancing and sat down beside her.

"What was it you said to Mrs. Fitzgerald, Mum, that made her go away?"

"I didn't make her go away, dear. She went because she was ready to go."

"But it was because of what you said. Why is that?"

"I don't know. I just made it up. Like the little songs you make up. It's something my gran would have said."

Mum had lived with her gran for a while after her parents had died in a car crash. Then she'd gone to live with her uncle Matt, who had been an important person in the Weatherman's Club. It was easy to forget that Mum had a whole life that happened before she became a Maloney.

"Sometimes I remember her voice, telling me stories, singing songs, chanting. Sometimes it's like she's still whispering in my ears, telling me things."

I wished Mum's gran would come whisper in *my* ear. I was always saying the wrong thing.

"You said you knew her—Mrs. Fitzgerald."

"No, Liz. I said I knew her *like*."

"How, Mum? How do you know her like? Is it because of your gran?"

"That's part of it," she said, and she sighed, put the mug down, and stretched her legs out in front of her. I crossed my legs and Neetch crept into my lap. Owen lay flat on his back and looked up at the sky. The clouds had yellow in them, like cloths that have been wiped across a dusty table.

"I remember," she said, and sighed and shook her head, and started again. "I remember the day the magicians from the Weathermen's Club all climbed into their cars and their vans and drove as fast as they could out of the city. It was early in the morning when the phone call came into the club. Uncle Matt had no one to mind me, so he put me in the back seat and took me with him. I'd been living with him for a few years by then, but I'd never seen anything like this. Everyone was in such a panic, and so angry. You'd think the world was going to end.

"We drove to a farm in the middle of nowhere—the Fitzgeralds are living there now, of course—and there was an old man and his son standing together in the yard, waiting for us. The old man was thin and gray, defeated and ashamed, and his son—your dad—no older than me, the same age as Neil is now, furious with everyone. The men from the club piled out of their cars and started shouting, and the old man stood there and said nothing, just a quiet word here and there, while the son yelled back and told them to leave him alone and it wasn't his fault. Then the Fitzgeralds showed up, that nasty little rat of a man and that scary, beautiful woman. My God, she hasn't aged a day! She stayed in the car while John-Joe tried to chase everyone away, but the old man and the boy had nowhere to go, so he gave them twenty-four hours to find a new home and clear out.

"Uncle Matt took charge. He sent some men to the well and sent others to scout around and others to ring estate agents and others to help the old man and the boy to pack. Oh, your dad was so strong. He protected his father as fiercely as any Shieldsman ever would or could. I liked him for that. I helped him pack his things and his father's things.

"The magicians found this house and the phone box and decided to move the Doorway. It was dangerous, but they were desperate and scared. They said it would only be for a while. They said they'd get the farm and the lake back as soon as they could. The spell nearly killed them, but it worked.

"Your dad and your granddad moved in here, of course, and I went back to Dublin, but the club was cracked and it didn't take much to break it. They no longer trusted the Weatherman, and the Weatherman no longer trusted them. The spell that moved the Door to the phone box left the magicians weak, and they never fully recovered their powers. It was as if they were being punished for what they did. Years went by, and the club lost power and influence bit by bit. The members grew old and retired, and there was no one to replace them. Uncle Matt bent and broke the rules and brought me in to help—that's how I ended up learning about magic and magic people and Mrs. Fitzgerald's sort. I loved it, but it was also sad because it was dying.

"Your granddad passed away and so did Uncle Matt. Your dad became the Weatherman. The men in charge of the club let me know that with Uncle Matt gone my help was neither needed nor welcome. But your Dad and I had kept in touch over the years, with letters and phone calls, and we used to visit each other and go on holidays together.

"He proposed to me one morning when the Spring arrived. There's nothing quite like the Spring—all the life and energy and warmth coming back into the world. When he went down on one knee and asked me to marry him I felt as if I were flying high over the world, bursting with happiness.

"I started the bed and breakfast because all of Uncle Matt's money vanished when Tony Holland robbed the club. Dad told you all about that, didn't he? How they blamed your dad for everything? They said Dad rang them and persuaded them to give Holland a job looking after their finances, and over five or six years Holland robbed them blind, then vanished. But Dad never rang them, though it's true he and Tony had been at school together. But Tony Holland's dad and John-Joe Fitzgerald were cousins— which makes me think . . . How long has she been planning this? And why?"

"She doesn't want to go back," I said. "She doesn't want to go back to the mountain—and they can't make her go back if she's the Weatherman, can they?"

"She came down from the mountain, married John-Joe, and persuaded him to steal the farm so she could be Weatherman," Mum said thoughtfully. "And when that didn't work she waited and waited and now she's ready."

"Because now she's got the Gray Thing!" I said. "They weren't able to do weather magic until they got the Gray Thing, and it must have taken them ages to work out how to get it free. But if she's all magical and powerful, why would she need weather magic?"

"Your dad won't go without a fight," Mum said. "She must know that. He's one of the four most powerful men in the world. It's just that he's not allowed to use that power much. But he will—to stop her—and even she might not be strong enough to fight him. The problem is, even if he wins, he loses . . ."

The sun burned through the yellow sky like a torch shining through a dirty sheet. The heat was massive, like dust burned in an oven and poured over everything. Every now and then one of the birds would drop from the wires or the roof or the trees and lie dead on the ground.

Mum went to check on Dad, and I sat on the grass and thought about things. I'd already known some of the story Mum had told me. She rarely talked about her mum and her dad. In fact, she almost never talked about when she was a kid—except when she was talking about her uncle Matt. Maybe she wanted to but didn't think I was ready. Maybe when I was older she'd tell me more, more about her mum and dad and about herself. My grandparents and young Mum—they kind of hung there at the back of the story, waiting, like spells, to change the way I looked at things.

What I wanted to do was to show Mum that I could change things, too—that even if I could never *be* Weatherman I was *good enough* to be Weatherman.

Neetch, who had deserted me to go fall asleep on Owen's stomach, suddenly jumped awake, trembling, as if from a bad dream. Owen stroked his back to calm him down, but he darted onto the grass and started to grow larger, digging his claws into the turf and leaning and pulling and twisting, as if something was dragging at him. He started to run in a wide arc, away from something and toward something at the same time.

"Neetch!" Owen shouted.

We could hear the grass under his claws, ripping and tearing. He spat and hissed and jumped from spot to spot as if bouncing on a trampoline. Then he braced his legs against the pull again, all his fur standing up and leaning in the direction of the road. He grew suddenly huge, so fast it was hard to see—a huge red shadow that tore free and leaped over the hedge and away.

But he had been hurt last night and he still wasn't better. Before he'd even cleared the hedge he was shrinking, and we heard him wail as whatever it was got hold of him again.

Owen and I ran through the gap in the hedge and followed Neetch around the field to the cattle track that led down to the road. He dashed across and jumped the hedge.

Between the hedge and the wood were the Ditches—a wee scrap of bog, wet and marshy, full of rushes and pools of oily black water, home to frogs and flies and a family of moorhens. There's a path through, but you have to jump from tussock to tussock and if you slip you can sink up to your knees in nasty gooey muck. The whole thing floods in really wet weather and we call it the swimming pool. The previous week's rain had drained down the hill or off the road, and the whole thing was now a cold wet mirror broken by grassy mounds and half-drowned willows.

I stopped when we reached the road. Neetch leaped from tussock to tussock, heading for the woods.

"We can't go there," I said, surprising myself. I was being sensible for Owen's sake, to hide how scared I was of meeting *her* in the woods.

Owen didn't care. "Neetch!" he called, and ran across the road and through the hedge and jumped from tussock to tussock.

"Owen!" I called, and glanced down toward the house. I could just see Dad's knees poking out in front of the Weatherbox. I could waste time trying to get his attention or I could pelt after Owen and drag him kicking and screaming back to the house before he got into trouble.

I crossed the road and the ditch and leaped from tussock to tussock after Owen, calling for both him and Neetch to come right back here at once or I'd tie them both to a flippin' tree and leave them there for the fairies to take. But they vanished out of the Ditches and into the woods, slipping away as if they were fairy things already, water and wild. My heart sank into my stomach because I knew I should go get Mum and Dad, but I also knew I didn't have time. Sometimes it's no good trying to be sensible, because you can't just let your little brother and his monster kitten go running off into the trees on their own.

I thought I'd catch Owen quickly, then drag him back to the house. Neetch could look after himself. I was wrong, though. Turns out Owen could move faster than a chicken with its tail feathers on fire, and he was small, running under branches and through thickets where I had to duck or go round. If he kept this up I'd have to get him to fill out an application form to join my Shieldsmen Club. Meantime I cursed and swore at his bobbing head and his vanishing back and his darting legs.

We climbed the hill, going in zigzags and sideways as Neetch, somewhere ahead, kept fighting against whatever it was pulling him on. Owen stopped running at the edge of a clearing, and I ran up behind him and took him by the arm, ready to carry him back over my shoulders if I had to.

I stopped. In all my running and jumping and chasing I had noticed without noticing that the woods were full of the strangest of sounds. It was like there was a whole orchestra playing, or more like a whole orchestra furiously fighting each other with their instruments. Or maybe it was the instruments that had decided they'd had enough and started playing the players so they screamed and wailed while the instruments cackled and laughed.

Hugh was there in the middle of the clearing, laughing, his arms spread out, conducting the horrible torture of the orchestra.

There were pillars all around the clearing, birch thin and tall as Hugh, and each pillar was a living thing and each living thing was weather. There was a whirlwind going round and round. There was a waterspout coming out of nowhere and digging into the ground, making a muddy hole and a foaming pool. There was a pillar of ice that crackled and creaked, another of blue-white light, too bright to look at, which crackled and sparked, and one of cloud that was a twisting black mist, which billowed and gushed. And there were many others—hazes and shimmers and fogs and snow.

"You're not supposed to be here," Hugh said. "The woods are mine. You can't come in here anymore without permission."

"What are you doing?" I asked.

"What your dad should have done years ago. Look at them—they're brilliant! And I'm only just getting started! I'll make them the size of mountains, big enough to flatten whole cities!"

132

"What? Why? Why would you want to do that? What would anyone want to flatten a flippin' city for?"

He looked at me as if I was speaking a foreign language.

"Because if you're strong, you have to show it to make everyone do what they're told!"

"But the Seasons won't let that happen. You'll be messing with the weather, and they hate that!"

"You're so stupid! I keep telling Mum how stupid you are! I don't know why she wants to keep you. I mean, look at you! Did you steal those shorts from that dumb brother of yours or from a charity shop? When you come to live with us all you'll be allowed to wear is a bin liner, and you can sleep in the doghouse, you hear? You'll be a scrawny chicken in a plastic bag."

I gaped at him.

"Live with you?" I blurted.

He laughed. "Yeah, you'd like that, wouldn't you? She thinks you can learn magic, but all you're good for is doing the dishes!"

"The only thing I'd do to the dishes is break them over your head! How do you think you can be Weatherman, Hugh? You can't even wash up after yourself! You can't even run a farm but you think you can run the world? Oh, you lot are good at stealing stuff all right, but what good is stealing stuff you don't know what to do with?"

Hugh glared and stuck his lower lip out and his face

133

went bright red. "You and your useless family! Looking down your noses at us and blaming us for losing your farm, which my dad got fair and square anyway. It's not our fault your granddad couldn't handle his money! Mum's right, your dad shouldn't be the Weatherman—your family don't deserve it. We do! And when we control the weather, we'll do what we like. People will pay us money for the weather they want, or we'll freeze them or boil them or sink them or wash them away! Nobody will mess with us and no one will be able to tell us what to do! We'll tell *them*!"

I couldn't believe what I was hearing.

"I knew it! You don't even know what the Weatherman does—or what he's supposed to do. You think he's like some sort of weather Santa Claus—going around making storms and sunshine or whatever he feels like. You're going to get everyone killed!"

"Oh, yeah? If that was true, then do you think I'd be able to make these?"

The columns had all slowed and thinned, going quiet while our shouting had got louder and louder, the rain and wind and lightning dying down to gentle drizzles and soft breezes and tiny flickers.

"I call them Weatherbots," Hugh said.

"Weatherbots?"

"Or Weathertrons."

I made a face. He made a face back.

"Names are hard," he said.

"Still, Weatherbots?"

"I'd like to see you do better."

"I could do better than that. *Owen* could do better than that. He'd call them Rainies, Foggies, Snowies, and Coldies, and even that'd be better than flippin' Weatherbots!"

"Fine, whatever. Shut up now."

"They're *elementals*, you ignorant flippin' eejit! Complex elementals that you've somehow built out of simple elementals, and the more complex elementals get the more dangerous they are! And you're trying to turn them into slaves or servants? That's wrong and stupid! You don't know what you're doing! Please let them go!"

"Oh, yeah? Whatever you call them, we knew enough to send one after your brother!"

"What?"

Hugh grinned.

"Oh my God, you didn't! Why would you *do* that?"

He laughed louder than ever.

"Dad was watching from the woods and saw the truck drive off. He told Mum, and Mum reckoned your cowardy custard dad was sending his little boy off all on his own to the Weathermen's Club. Well, he won't find much there, and if he's smart he'll turn around and come straight back, but if he goes to AtmoLab? Kablooey!"

"Don't you dare! Nobody kablooeys my brother! Wait, where's Owen?"

I looked around, and saw something beyond the clearing. I moved past Hugh, who followed with his repulsive grin.

Standing a little way along the path was Mrs. Fitzgerald, in a black dress with her black hair long and smooth around her face, smiling at me as I walked up warily. Owen was standing in front of her, glaring, rigid with rage and frustration, his arms stiff by his sides.

"Liz! Tell her to let Neetch go!"

"Owen, come away! Come on, quick!" I pointed at Mrs. Fitzgerald. "You! Leave my brother alone!"

She raised her eyebrows. "I'm not doing anything to your brother, dear."

"Give me back Neetch!" yelled Owen.

"Not Owen, Neil!"

"Oh, him. He should be fine, for the time being, so long as he doesn't go where he shouldn't."

"Stop it! Call it back!"

"Too late, I'm afraid. Much too late."

"Please!"

"I think you should go home now. Take your brother and go. Your parents will need you. You can comfort them and they can comfort you. Things are about to get very busy, and you should try to make the most of what time

136

there is left. When all this is over and done, everything will have changed, Liz."

She sounded almost sad as she said this, her eyes far away, her voice soft, like Mum's when she's telling Owen a story, just as he's falling asleep.

"What do you mean?"

"I will bring a Season of the world like no other—a Season beyond all imagining. I will break every law of man and nature into pieces and remake them to my own liking. My Season, Liz. But first, the Weatherman will fall, and everything and everyone you've ever known will fall with him. I'm sorry, but I will not go back. I will never sing again. I will end the world first."

Her presence was like a physical force pressing down on me. I could barely breathe.

"I won't . . ." I started to say, and stopped. My mouth was dry. "I won't be your hostage. Or . . . or your apprentice."

She seemed to come back to herself, and smiled brightly. "Oh, my dear, but of course. I understand. I was wrong to try and drag you away from your family. Don't worry. When the time is right you'll come to me. There'll be nobody else left."

"No!"

She looked at me. Her gray eyes never blinked and the smile on her lips never touched them. Nothing in the world ever seemed to touch her. She was so strong and sure. I longed to be that strong and sure. Nobody would ever call me mad again, and, if they did, I wouldn't care. Nobody could ever hurt me if I was like her.

"Come on, we're going. Owen, come on!"

"Not without Neetch!

"Oh, for God's sake! Where is—Oh!"

It was right beside me, standing just to my left and her right. It was so thin and gray and still, it had basically camouflaged itself against all the trees and bushes. The Gray Thing that had been such a weird mess on the floor of the barn had grown twice as tall as Mrs. Fitzgerald, even hunched over and crouched the way it was. Its body and its arms and its legs were as thin as hosepipes, and its hands and its feet were long and graceful. Its face was a sort of stretched oval shape on top of its neck, and its eyes and its mouth were the same: black hollows that barely moved or changed but were sometimes sad and sometimes angry and always scary. It had sort of hair that stuck out like branches of a tree or icicles from the back of its head, and it was holding its hands cupped together to make a cage. Curled up in the cage, shivering and shaking, still a kitten, the scars on his face livid, was Neetch.

"Let him go!" I said.

Mrs. Fitzgerald shook her head, no longer smiling. "No," she said. "He's a long way from home. Like me. I want to know what he's doing here and how he got here. When I'm finished, I might let you have whatever is left. He's only a filthy old bog beast. I was never that fond of the nasty thing."

Owen wailed. I took a step back.

How was I different from her? I wanted to be like her. I wanted to have her power and her control and her freedom to be whatever she wanted to be. But if I was like her, would I do the things she did?

How was I different?

For a start, I wouldn't leave a friend behind, even if I had to take Owen's word for the "friend" part. I already felt bad enough about the poor Gray Thing. Could that weird, crooked creature really be a whole new Season? Had Mrs. Fitzgerald really made a baby Season her slave? Years trapped under the water, and now this? And if this was a Season, she was using it to make slaves of the elementals for Hugh to play with, to send after my brother. My mind was flat with rage. It wasn't fair. It wasn't right. I wouldn't let her do it to anyone else—not even the wretched cat. I steadied myself.

"You'd better start running, Owen," I said. "Go! Now!"

He hesitated, then ran across the clearing, into the trees and down the hill. I had my bow in my hand. I drew the arrow and loosed before I really thought about what I was doing. If I had thought, I think she would have read it in me.

The arrow flew at Hugh, who never even saw it coming.

CHAPTER 15

NEIL

We caught one of the electric trams to the canal. Then we walked across a bridge and down the towpath until we reached a strange and disturbing building. The corporate headquarters of AtmoLab Inc. were a sort of metal and glass shape, like a giant letter of the alphabet that had been melted and twisted until you couldn't quite work out what the letter had been. We walked between a pair of huge black cars parked in front of the entrance with trunks open wide like the jaws of a weird, deep-sea fish and the insides full of metal boxes and wires. The doors slid open on their own, and the cold of the air-conditioning froze the sweat in my shirt and made me shiver. Our shoes clattered loudly on the polished floor of the lobby, echoing up and down so it sounded as if there were an army of caterpillars in big brown boots tramping around.

There was a pile of boxes and cables and electronic equipment to one side. As we went past the pile, a short, plump man with a beard and a pair of round glasses crossed our path, arms outstretched, carrying something heavy and expensive-looking from the pile to the car. He gave us a nod as he went past.

A tall thin man in a colorful shirt and shorts that came down to his knees hurried after, arguing with a glum-looking woman in a blue dress. They both had iPads in their hands.

Behind the reception desk there was a security guard whose main job seemed to be to disapprove of everything that happened in the lobby. His peaked cap was pulled low over his forehead, almost hiding his eyes, his thick lips were curled downwards as though he had weights hanging off the ends of them, and his shoulders were bunched up nearly as far as his ears. He looked at Ed. Ed nudged me.

"We're here to see Mr. Holland," I said, trying not to squeak. "Tell him we're from the Weatherman."

The security guard held up his own iPad, peered at it closely, glowered at me, swiped it once or twice with a thick finger, then gave a grunt and a single, short nod.

"Thank you!" said Ed. The guard glared at him and led us to the elevators.

"I love the way all the doors in Dublin just slide open for you," said Ed, his voice booming out through the empty air. I saw the security guard flinch, ever so slightly. The elevator pinged and the doors opened.

"See!" said Ed, and we went in.

"Maybe we should have called home," I said as the elevator rose.

"What would we tell them? We don't know what the story is and there's still no sign of the Shieldsmen. Honestly, the worst that can happen is the boy Holland has us thrown out by Mr. Personality there. Your mum and dad have enough on their minds without us calling every five minutes."

"I suppose," I said.

The doors opened again three floors later, and we wandered down a corridor until we came to a door with the name *Tony Holland* written on it. I knocked.

Mr. Tony Holland, CEO and senior managing director of AtmoLab Inc., sat behind a small desk covered in black leather, leaning back in a large leather seat with his stockinged feet up on the desk. He was sipping from an extremely large take-out cup of coffee and nibbling a muffin, occasionally brushing a few crumbs onto the deep, soft, beige carpet. His dark hair was streaked with gray and tied back in a long ponytail. He wore jeans and a shirt, no tie. On the desk there was yet another iPad, as well as a laptop, a big, wide desktop monitor, and three cell phones.

He was about my dad's age. Of course he was. They'd been in the same class at school. Dad had told me all about Tony Holland. Well, not about him being in the country and CEO of AtmoLab—this was new. Dad had assumed he'd vanished to some faraway tax haven in the Caribbean.

Tony Holland finished his muffin, sipped his coffee, wiped his fingers and his lips on a napkin, swung his feet off the desk, and sat forward.

"So," he said, "you're Maloney's boy, are you? And who's your friend?"

He looked like a jet-setting entrepreneur, but he had the broad, thick accent of a Midlands farmer.

"This is Ed Wharton," I said. "He's . . . a tourist."

"Yeah? That's nice. How's your dad?"

"Fine," I said.

"I'll bet he is. He must be fair beside himself right now, I'd say. It's weird, you know, but all this time I've been expecting him to come charging through that door with a gang of cops to arrest me and throw me in jail. Now it's too late, and he sends you instead. He's a queer sort of man, your father."

I looked at Ed, then took a step forward, breathing deeply. "You stole the money," I said.

Tony Holland's eyebrows shot up. "Of course I stole the money! What else was I going to do? When that woman turns up at me door and tells me I'd better do it or else, I don't wait to see what the 'or else' is!"

"Woman? Mrs. Fitzgerald? She told you to do it?"

"Of course she did! I'm no thief, but you don't want to cross that woman. Look, John-Joe's a cousin of me dad's, but none of us liked him. We couldn't believe it when she married him. A young one like her and a twisted curse of a yoke like Fitzy? Well, we soon found out. Say a word about her, look at her funny, ask the wrong question and cows'll sicken, money'll be lost, folks'll fall down stairs and break bones. I'm no crook, but I'll be as crooked as a politician's expenses to keep her away from my family."

"So she threatened you?" I asked.

"Threatened me?" he gave a bitter laugh. "Oh, you could say that she threatened me, all right. I got a lump, you know. Under me arm, here. Big and round and nasty as you please. Went to the doctor and had it tested. Malignant, it was. Well that's me done for, says I. Made my peace with God and got ready as best I could for the long fall. Then one night she comes up to the house, walks in like she owns the place, aye, and everyone in it, and she lays it all out. Her big plan. For me to go work for the Weathermen's Club, strip it bare, then set up a corporation and buy it out. 'I've news for you,' I tells her. 'Sounds like you need a con man, not an accountant. Sounds like you need someone who has more than a year to live.' 'Get it tested again,' she tells me. 'They'll tell you it's benign, and you'll wake up one morning and it'll be gone, and you'll do as I tell you or it'll come back, and if it comes back, it'll be back to stay. And if you're feeling brave and honorable, then let me tell you I've a set— one for each of your family.' Well, I thinks about it for all of about five seconds before I says to her, 'You're the boss.'"

"Dear God," said Ed.

"But," I said, "the club, afterward—they said Dad had rung them up and told them to give you the job! They heard his voice! They blamed him!"

"Good God, lad, don't you think she can do voices over the phone? She could do the flippin' Pope if she wanted to, to the Pope's mother and the Pope in the same room as his old mum, and the poor woman still wouldn't be sure which was which!" He was flushed and angry, and his eyes were haunted, but full of fierce energy.

"Don't think," he said, pointing a finger at me. "Don't think for a second I won't put my family before yours. Don't think for a second I'll go against her now. You run on home and pack up your things and move out and never look back, and that'll be the end of it! You hear me? I want this over and I want it done and I want my life back."

The poor guy was weeping now, big tears flowing down his cheeks. I wondered how long he'd been keeping this pent up inside him, waiting for my dad to burst in so he could confess it all. In the end I'd do just as well as my dad, I supposed.

"So you bankrupted the club, is that right?" said Ed.

"Took every penny," Holland confirmed with a nod and a sniff and a touch of professional pride. He wiped his face dry. "Sold off every treasure in their vaults, ransacked every bank account, shifted it all offshore. Never touched a penny myself."

He slapped the desk with an open palm. "Not a penny went into me own pocket. Blood money, it was! Cursed!"

"And all the members left or died?"

"Retired in disgrace, living out their lives in old folk's homes. I'm sorry for them. I'm not proud of it. But I did what had to be done."

"So what is AtmoLab, then?" Ed asked.

Holland leaned back in his chair and looked up at Ed and licked his lips. "It's the club," he said. "It's the club— its charter, its assets and responsibilities, all wrapped in a new corporate identity. That's what AtmoLab is. We own it all. We own the bed and breakfast and we own the phone box, and today we're going down and we're taking possession."

"For her," I said, sick to my stomach.

"Aye, I'll be handing the whole lot over to her. She can do what she likes with it. I'll be out. I'll be free and clear."

"You can't do this!" I wailed.

He wasn't crying now. He glared at me as if I were a whole new species of fool that had just crawled up out of his carpet.

"It's done," he said. "It's all over and there'll be no going back and no stopping her, so just get out before you get hurt."

"You don't understand!" I tried.

"I understand better than you!" he roared. "You think we don't know all about the Weathermen down our way? We knew all about the old well, and your blasted grandfather who let all this happen! We know more than we want to about the Seasons coming and going! So let it happen. Who cares if it's Maloneys or Fitzgeralds in charge? It's all the same! It'll be a lot safer in her hands than it would be in yours, that's for sure!"

"But the Shieldsmen—"

"That's enough! Get out, now, go on. Go home and pack your things and be safe, far away from the likes of her and from all of this."

"We'll go," said Ed, putting a hand on my shoulder. "I was just wondering—you say you own the phone box?"

Holland waved a hand dismissively. "It's complicated. Technically, the State owns it, and it's protected as a heritage site, but we have a sort of leasehold over it to run it and maintain it."

147

"And the phone line?"

Holland looked up at him sharply. "Yeah," he said. "We own the line, too. You would not believe the amount of time and money and influence we spent gaining ownership of that line, but we got it."

"Recently?"

"Yes. This summer."

"And did you leave the line connected?"

"No," he said. "No, we disconnected it prior to upgrading. Back in July, it was."

"You disconnected the Weatherbox?" My voice was a high-pitched shriek. "That's why it won't ring!"

He sat back in his chair and stared at me defiantly. "Yes. She told me to, so I did it."

"Can you reconnect it? Can you?" I asked.

"If I wanted." He snapped his fingers. "Just like that."

"Then do it! Do it before something awful happens!"

"If I do, something awful *will* happen—to me and my family. You don't want something awful to happen to you and yours? Leave. You and your family leave. I won't say it again. I won't tell you to get out again, either."

"Come on," Ed said, and he guided me out of the office and let the door swing shut behind us. I had to lean on the wall for a moment. I felt weak and hot and then weak and cold.

"You OK?" asked Ed.

"No," I said miserably, "I'm not."

Ed pressed the button to summon the elevator. An arrow went red and numbers began to slide up the display beside the door. I felt the skin on the back of my neck begin to prickle. I looked up at the ceiling, then down at the floor. The doors slid open.

"Wait," I said. "Wait!"

I put my hands out to block Ed from getting in.

"What is it?"

"There's something . . . There's something . . ."

Down in the far left corner of the elevator there was a shadow. With the fluorescent light on overhead and nothing at all to cast it, there should have been no shadow—and yet there was. Coiled like a snake ready to strike. And there was a tiny flash, like an ember flaring in the ashes of a dead fire.

"Can you see it?" I asked.

"See what?" said Ed

The doors slid shut.

"Let's take the stairs," I said. "And let's hurry."

"Are you sure?"

"No," I said. "Let's do it anyway."

We went back down the corridor, past Tony Holland's door, and found the stairs and headed down. I felt like an idiot. I was spooked and upset and seeing things.

We had reached the second landing when we heard

something on the stairs above. We froze and looked up, but couldn't see anything or anyone. We held our breath. Except for the roar of the air conditioner, the stairwell was silent.

All the hairs on my arm were standing up.

"Run," I said.

We ran. Down the third flight, around and down, and into a wall of air that was so warm it was almost hot. The stairwell went dark as the lights above either went out or were blocked by something big and thick and heavy. The hot air and the cold mingled, the hot air going up, the cool air coming down.

"Hurry!" I gasped. The word was snatched from my lips by a sudden gust of wind. Cobwebs and papers and balls of dust were floating around us like eerie alien fish in some strange unearthly current.

I glanced back and saw a shape on the landing above. It stood like a human, with arms and legs as thin as sticks all drawn in jagged lines. There was an inhuman face with wicked, angry eyes and a grinning mouth that opened wider and wider. A torrent of mist and rain poured through it.

It was an elemental. In a building. Making weather.

Fat drops stung my face. More and more rain was lashed down at us by the driving wind, soaking us completely.

"Come on," said Ed. "I hate getting wet."

Sheltering as best I could under Ed the walking umbrella, I moved away from the wall, grabbed the handrail, and began to pull myself down the second-to-last flight of stairs.

Gallons of foaming water came rushing down the stairs. Soon, the flow was up to our knees and still rising.

How were they, how was *it*, doing this? It'd need hot air and cold air and lots and lots of water. And yet it didn't seem to be in any danger of running out. Water kept rising on the steps, and more and more was falling in sheets and curtains from the flights above, down through the open core of the stairwell.

And then I realized that it was the air conditioning! Of course an office block like this had air conditioning, and air conditioners are machines for heating and cooling air and moving that air around. There would also be water: for the cafeteria, for cleaning, for the toilets. That's what the elemental was working with. It could probably tap the mains supply for the whole city! It might have been draining the flippin' canal outside, for all I knew.

So it had energy, hot and cold air, and water. Lots and lots of water. Some of that water might be from the toilets. Gah.

"Oh, no," I said. "Look at that."

The last flight was nearly swamped, and the water was halfway up the door to the lobby. The sound of running water echoed in the narrow walls and up and down the stairwell. Somewhere an alarm was ringing. Something started to laugh, and a white wave poured down on us. We just about had the chance to scream before we were swept off our feet.

Oh, I thought. *Drowning. I know how to do this. I've had practice.*

Then I was thrown and tossed, twisted and turned. I went up and down, up and down. I saw bubbles, millions of tiny little bubbles, most of them coming out of me, and mostly I just felt cold.

Down there, everything was calm. I saw the stairs and the door and a pair of kicking legs. I shook my head, the last few bubbles bursting from my mouth. I forced my arms and legs to move and tried to work out which way was up. I knew it should have been obvious but somehow it wasn't. My limbs felt weak and feeble, and my chest felt as though someone was parking a car on top of it. A strong hand grabbed me by the hair and pulled. It was much more painful than the car. I broke the surface, gasped, spat, and roared. The hand let go.

"Gaaaah!" I said. "Gaaaaaah!"

"All right?" yelled Ed in my ear. "Stay up this time!"

"Gaahahahaaaa!" I said, moving my arms and legs in a desperate struggle to stay afloat. *I should probably kick off my shoes,* I thought.

"Now, hang on!" he yelled. "Be with you in a minute!"

He took a deep breath and dived.

I pushed my face back below the surface and saw the stairs and the door. There was Ed, both hands on the door handle, both feet against the jamb. The door crept open an inch, and then another.

The water in the stairwell began to turn, sweeping me around, sucking me down like the whirlpool in a bath. My wail of fear cut off as I went under one final time. Ed was holding the door open against the weight of the water, fighting the pressure. It was rushing past him and through the door at terrific speed. I hit the door sideways and got stuck, the flow of the water trying to break me in two. Ed took hold of my leg and pulled me down and pushed me like a postman shoving a package into a tiny letterbox. The water carried me through, scraping me against the edges of the doorway, and I was spat out onto the floor of the AtmoLab lobby.

I let the water carry me along the smooth, polished floor until I finally washed up in a heap beside the elevators. With a gentle squelch Ed drifted to a stop beside me. We coughed and spat and groaned. More water flowed through the open door, flooding through the lobby, before the door shut completely.

"What are you doing? What are you doing? What have you done?"

The security guard tried to stride angrily toward us, but it was difficult because he was splashing clumsily through a fast, shallow stream that came up to his ankles.

Ed and I were dazed and exhausted. We helped each other slosh to our feet and stood there, dripping and blinking and shaking our heads, while the security guard demanded to know what was going on. At the other side of the lobby, the bearded man, the thin man, and the woman in the blue dress were scurrying about trying to save their equipment.

"I'm calling the police! Wreckers! Vandals!" The security guard splashed back to his desk. Then he stopped and gave a wail and fished his iPad out of the water, holding it up by a corner with his thumb and forefinger.

"Do you see that?" he yelled. "Do you see that?"

"Should have done a backup!" called the woman in the blue dress.

"The backup's under me desk, Cherie! The backup's waterlogged! Everything's waterlogged!"

We ignored them and concentrated on wading slowly but steadily toward the exit.

"Do you know what's happening?" asked the small man with the beard popping up before us, shaking water from something that looked delicate and expensive before tossing it over his shoulder.

"Elemental," I said. "There's an elemental in the stair-well."

The security guard stiffened. "A what now?" he said and took a step toward the door. It creaked and groaned. He took a step back.

"The elemental," Ed explained, "has filled the stairwell with what must by now be hundreds of gallons of water. Any second now—"

"An elemental?" broke in Cherie. "Wow! What's that?"

"Derived from the four elements, lass," said the man in the shorts. "Earth, air, fire, water. Elementals are sup-posed to be made of or capable of controlling the elements, you see?"

"I know that, Bob!" said Cherie.

"Load o' nonsense," said the man with the beard.

"Be quiet a minute, Clive," said Cherie, waving him away and bearing down on me with a slightly terrifying enthusiasm. "Is that what you're saying is on the stairs? An elemental? That would be awesome!"

"Uh, maybe?" I said. "Kind of? I mean, yes."

There were more cracks and groans and a kind of gur-gling. Ed and I were getting nervous and anxious to be on our way, but the three scientists were in front of us, and the security guard was behind us.

"Ah, don't mind them, they're clearly in shock," said

Clive, gesturing toward us. "The pipes have burst, obviously."

"Is that it?" the security guard demanded. "Did you burst the pipes? You've the whole place destroyed!"

"No, listen!" said Cherie. "Didn't Holland say something about controlling the weather one time? We all laughed, but I think this is tied in to the project, you know—the phone box and all. This is amazing!"

Clive rolled his eyes. "It's hard enough keeping things on a scientific footing without all this mystical rubbish creeping in. We'll never be able to publish any credible findings at this rate."

Creak. Crack. Groan. Gurgle. Hiss.

"Don't mind us," I said. "Come on, Ed."

"I think you should leave, too," Ed told them as we pushed through the scientists and headed for the exit. "I don't know how much longer that door'll hold."

"You're not going anywhere!" said the security guard, taking long, leaping strides through the water until he was blocking our way. "Stay right there, you, you pipe bursters, you!"

"Is the big bad elemental going to come and eat us all up?" said Clive with a laugh.

"It's trying to eat Neil and me all up, actually," Ed told him. "But I don't think it cares who else it eats on the way.

156

Hey!" Bob had started moving cautiously toward the door. "I really wouldn't do that!"

Bob looked over his shoulder at us.

"It's either burst pipes, or a hitherto undiscovered species capable of manipulating energy and matter. One way or another, I've got to know."

"Could you please get back to salvaging the equipment?" demanded Clive with exasperation. "We don't have time for this nonsense!"

"Just a peek!" said Bob.

"I'm not so sure, Bob," said Cherie.

"Nobody! Move!" yelled the security guard. Everybody looked at him. "Nobody moves until we get to the bottom of this!"

"Look," I said. "We need to get out of here. That door's going to—"

The door exploded, dissolving in a spray of splinters. The deluge surged out. We were swept off our feet and sent rolling into the pile of equipment. Boxes tumbled and bobbed around us. I was pushed up against one of the tinted windows that lined the wall of the lobby.

The elemental came howling through the doorway in a blast of fog and rain that churned the choppy waters of the lobby into a frenzy. Whitecapped waves rolled over the pile of equipment and more sharp-edged stuff flew at us and at the windows. The glass cracked and splintered without breaking. I splashed and kicked and thrashed with my arms to stay afloat, fending off heavy boxes and tangling loops of wire and all sorts of big metal things that were bobbing crazily around me.

The clouds swirled around the center of the lobby, turning like a cyclone, going from white to gray to dark to black. Blue-white flashes lit them from the inside. The waves were being whipped higher and higher. Ed, the guard, and the three scientists were clinging together in a sort of human raft. The storm was working its way up to a hurricane, and then to whatever it is that's worse than a hurricane. We had to get out.

The bare metal legs of a chair gleamed under the tossing waves. I grabbed the chair by a leg, then fought to get my feet under me and stand steady in the heaving water. The wind whipped around me and waves tried to swamp me, rising up to my chin, then pulling away and then rolling back again. In the gap between rolling and pulling I swung the chair with all my strength and smashed it into the window. It didn't do much. In fact, it barely scratched the surface. Never mind. Wave up, wave down, and swing. *Crash*. Again. Again. Nothing but scratches.

The others must have got the idea, because as I drew back to swing again, they came out of the waves like bedraggled merpeople with boxes and computer monitors.

Clive had what looked like a very thick book—a technical manual of some sort. When he threw it, the pages fluttered and it stuck to the window and slid down. The box and the computer monitor and another chair did more damage. The glass cracked and bulged.

The waves were getting higher now, knocking us off our feet and threatening to suck us into the middle of the lobby—where we'd survive about as long as a snowflake in a furnace. We had to grab each other to stop ourselves from being washed away. I really, really hoped that the workers on the upper floors had the good sense to stay where they were, or that there was a fire escape that would take them out the back. We were getting weaker by the minute.

Then Ed and the guard rose out of the foam with a big metal bench held over their heads. With an enormous heave and a pair of mighty roars they sent it smashing into the window like a spear or a battering ram. The window didn't so much break as fall out of its frame and collapse onto the grass outside. Water poured out, and we poured out with it, pulling each other along until we were away from the glass and the water and the wind, on warm dry grass, in the sunshine. We fell together, heaving great gasps of air and shivering in our soaked clothes, while the storm vented through the broken window like a high-pressure leak from a hosepipe full of weather.

"It'll . . . it'll blow . . . blow itself out . . . soon . . ." I said, between gasps. "I hope."

I scanned the park and the road and the canal in case there were more elementals hanging around. I could see lots of curious onlookers staring at AtmoLab, and four or five big men in colorful sweaters and red skirts strolling across the grass. No elementals.

Ed was lying on his back, arms and legs splayed wide, breathing rapidly.

"Everyone . . . OK?" he asked.

None of us were OK, not really, but we might get to OK with rest and warm dry clothes and only a little bit of medical attention. Maybe one of the big men in the colorful sweaters and skirts who were getting nearer and nearer would turn out to be a doctor. That would be nice.

A shadow fell across us, and a friendly male voice spoke. "All right, by?"

I looked up in surprise. "Not really."

The five men in colorful sweaters and red skirts, which I suppose were actually kilts, stood around us in a semicircle. They were all smiling.

"A little birdie told us we should stop by, by. What are ye all wet for, by? Did ye go swimmin' or what? What'd ye go swimmin' for, like?"

"You look like me auntie's cat after it fell in the Lough that time, by," another one said.

"What the hell were you doin' throwin' the poor cat round the Lough for, anyway, by?"

"Sure the cat loved it! Just me aim was put off when me auntie fired the flippin' shotgun at one of the ducks, like. She hated them ducks, by."

"There's always a flippin' duck to blame with you, isn't there?"

"Hello?" I said.

"Howaye, by?"

"What little birdie? Who?" I said. My voice came as though from a far-off world, a world of ghosts and spirits. My voice sounded like the voice of a ghost. I began to get worried.

"Never mind that now, by. Just tell us which of you is the Weatherman, all right? The big man wants to see him."

"But," I said. "No, you see, that's my dad. He sent me to . . . he sent me up here to . . . er, who are you?"

"Plenty of time for tellin', by. So it's you, is it?"

"Hey," said Ed. "What are you doing?"

"Never you mind, by," said one of the men. "Stay where you are, like, OK?"

"All right, like," said another one. "We haven't got all day, by."

Five bulky shapes stooped and strong hands grabbed my arms and legs. I was raised off the ground. My weak protests and struggles were ignored. They carried me away across the grass, swinging between them like a sack of grain. I twisted my head and saw Ed rising, soaked and slow, hand outstretched after me, face contorted in terror. I could tell what he was thinking.

He was thinking about what Mum was going to do to him when she found out he'd lost me.

CHAPTER 16

LIZ

Mrs. Fitzgerald's hand lashed out, quicker than a striking snake. The arrow jumped off its path, vanishing into a clump of nettles. I took the bow by one end, raised it over my head, and smashed it down on the hands in which the Gray Thing was holding Neetch.

It snatched its hands back, and made a sound like an animal or a bird, or like rain falling a certain way. It was a sound like nothing I'd ever heard—a gasp of hurt and puzzlement and betrayal. How could this be a Season, a mighty and powerful being, one of the great spirits of the skies? It was older than me, but maybe, for a Season, it was still just a baby.

"I'm sorry, Baby Season!" I whispered. I felt like I'd just kicked a puppy.

Neetch fell to the ground, landing with all his feet

churning. He tore off like a small red cannonball across the clearing, to the sound of claws ripping through greenery. I sprinted along behind him, slinging my bow back over my shoulder.

Now I could feel her at my back, feel her reaching for me, black hair blowing wild around a face white as bleached bone, dress billowing like huge black wings. I didn't bother to turn around to see if she was really there. If I'd made her angry, we could be in real trouble. I'd fired an arrow at her son. She was probably furious. Worse still, maybe it was all for nothing. She had managed to force Neetch to come all the way up here against his will. All she had to do now was call him back again. Maybe the two hags below were awake now. Maybe they'd noticed their pet missing. Maybe they'd call him back to them.

I caught up with Owen and slowed down to stay behind him. Neetch was darting along the path ahead of him, stopping every few seconds to let Owen catch up.

Behind us, I heard rustling and crunching, as something big slipped through the trees and down the path. I grabbed Owen's shoulder, pulling him off the path and behind a tree. The Baby Season went past, searching, its head lowered, turning this way and that, its black eyes peering up and down. Neetch leaped out of a bush and Owen and me followed him.

The Baby Season stopped and turned, swinging around after us, moving gracefully and easily.

"Neetch!" I yelled desperately. "Get big! It'll squash us!"

Neetch didn't, though. Maybe he couldn't because he was still too hurt after last night. He zigged and zagged ahead of us, leading the way through the trees. The Baby Season was moving fast on its long bendy legs, barely touching the branches or the leaves overhead or the undergrowth below as it went, stepping carefully, bending away from and around anything in its way. It was right on top of us.

I skidded to a stop, my sneakers raising a shower of dirt and twigs and leaves, grabbed a long crooked stick from the ground, and swung it wildly at the Baby Season. It was wet and rotten and fell apart in my hands. The Baby Season caught me and lifted me up, cupping me in its palm.

Its skin was warm and soft and bendy, like a rubber band. Its fingers wrapped around me and held me tight, lifting me up like a waiter holding a tray of food over his head as he moved through a crowd. It was carrying me back to the path. Back to her. It was me it had been sent after, not Owen or Neetch. Swinging and swaying, way up where the tops of the trees all crowded together, I spat and screamed, not because I thought anyone would come and save me, but because I did not want to die quietly. If the worst I could do was give the enemy a splitting headache, well, so be it.

When I paused to take a breath between screams, I heard something come ripping through the canopy. Neetch, leaping from tree to tree, a screeching streak of red, legs splayed, claws gleaming, mouth spread to show his teeth, plunged down into the Gray Thing's head and began to rip and tear. The Baby Season stopped, shuddered, and screamed, groping for Neetch with its free hand. A stone crashed into its shoulder. I saw Owen below on the path, bringing his arm back for another shot.

I grabbed a finger and pushed, bending it back and back until if it had been one of my fingers it would have been broken and I'd have been on my way to the hospital to get a splint put on it. The Baby Season didn't like it. It was pulling Neetch away from its face and trying to dodge Owen's stones at the same time. It shook its hand, the hand with me in it, and flung me away, out into the air over the path, with a long way down to fall.

I heard Owen shout.

I tried to scream. I had no breath. Nothing to grab hold of. Nothing to land on. The ground came up with sickening speed.

I landed on a flying carpet.

Landing on the ground would probably have been softer. Under the red carpet were thick, hard muscles that moved and bunched and flexed. I grabbed handfuls of fur and held tight, and Neetch landed feet first on the path. I lost my grip and rolled down his flank to hit the ground after all. I couldn't even groan. Owen was tugging at my arm. It hurt.

"Come on! Come on! It's coming!"

It wasn't just coming. It was standing right there over us. Its eyes and its mouth wide and black like something wild and howling and hungry. There was no escaping that. Not for me anyway.

"Run," I said to Owen. "Get away. Go!"

"Come on!" he said, and kept pulling.

I forced myself upright, if only to push him under a bush or something. He pulled me toward Neetch.

Neetch was crouched low, waiting for us to climb on his back. He was the size of a horse, trembling with tiredness.

I hoisted Owen up and threw myself over, barely managing to grab some fur before Neetch was off and running.

Riding a cat is not like riding a horse. Horses have those long legs and big barrel-shaped bodies. Even barebacked, it's all about gripping with your legs and, like, rolling with the movements of the horse. Cats have short legs and all their power comes from their flanks and their haunches. It's like riding a bag of angry stoats. Every movement tries to throw you off in a different direction, and cats don't run straight. They're always speeding up and slowing down, and they sort of crackle with static electricity, and if they're being chased through a wood by a magic monster it's even worse than that. Still, it was better than the Baby Season and *her*. So we hung on.

Neetch ran down the path away from the Gray Thing. Owen and me bounced so hard our legs came loose from around his sides and we were hanging on just by the handfuls of fur. He didn't like that and screeched in pain, and we didn't like it and screeched in terror. The Baby Season was not as fast as Neetch, but those long bendy legs kept it right behind us, lashing at us with those weird fingers, punching trees and pulling out small bushes and tearing up thorny undergrowth in frustration. Neetch jumped and leaped and howled and dodged and hopped and climbed. All this time we were slipping down his back and down his sides, trailing our legs, bouncing them painfully off hard things and through soft things.

But no matter how much he jumped and leaped and dodged he couldn't get ahead of the Baby Season's long legs and long hands. They kept blocking him off, herding him in and out. We were going around and around in circles. It stooped down and reached for us, its arms and hands all tangled now with ivy and briars and broken branches. Owen let go of Neetch's fur and slid down his back. I grabbed the collar of his shirt. He dangled behind us like an extra tail.

And Neetch started to shrink.

He was tiring fast. I could hear his breathing becoming more labored, feel the weakness in his muscles and in the way he slumped every time he paused. Now he was pony-sized, staggering and limping. The fur I was holding on to was coming loose. My arm was in agony.

Neetch was big-dog-sized now. Without letting go, I let my legs slide down and tried to sort of run alongside him. He went from big-sized dog to medium-sized dog and both my shins bashed into a root. I let go. Neetch tripped and fell with me. Owen rolled along with us, and we all slipped and slid and rolled, and when we came to a stop we were out from under the Baby Season, lying in a heap on the path. I could see the boggy pools of the Ditches through a gap ahead. Behind us the Baby Season was bent over, turning this way and that, searching for us.

I pushed Owen down the path and picked up the tiny mewling Neetch. He was so small I could have slipped him into my pocket.

Ignoring the pain and the tiredness, we ran down the path, out from amongst the trees, and into the Ditches. I didn't bother with the tussocks. I knew where the highest parts were and the flooded paths. I splashed right through, hopping over places where I thought the deeper holes were. I could see the hedge and the road. Nearly there. Nearly there.

By now the Baby Season had worked out that we weren't underfoot. It turned to give chase with a long honk like a goose or a hunting horn. It came crashing out of the woods and into the bog behind us, taking great long strides that ate up the distance, sending ripples like waves rolling across the flood. We had seconds.

I turned away from the road and took three long, loping leaps to the left, landing on a tiny, muddy island of heather and reeds. Right in front of that island should be the deepest bog hole in the county—or so they said. I stopped and handed Neetch to Owen and stood in front of them with my arms spread wide.

"Come on, then!" I screamed.

The Baby Season took another step, sending bog water flooding over the island and around my legs. Its left foot landed in the bog hole, and sank. It tried to pull it out, stumbled, and its right foot went into the hole. That sank, too, right down. It waved its hands to keep its balance as it pulled and struggled and heaved, sloshing black mucky water all over us, but sinking deeper and deeper. It pushed down with its hands, and they sank down into the mud and became stuck. Its face was scared and confused now, its long stiff hair, all wreathed in ivy and thorns from the chase in the woods, was bending from side to side as it shook its great head and let out a long wail of fear.

I wondered then why, it if was a Season of some sort, it

didn't use weather to get out of the bog hole, and why it hadn't used weather to catch us. A strong wind or a block of ice or a blast of lightning would have stopped us before we'd gone ten yards. I guessed that Mrs. Fitzgerald wouldn't even let it do that, keeping it as her slave, keeping the weather for herself and Hugh.

"OK," I said, and I carefully backed away from it. I picked up Neetch and caught Owen by the arm.

"But the poor thing!" Owen wailed.

"Shut up," I told him. "You were pelting rocks at it a minute ago."

When you defeat a monster you're supposed to feel triumphant and brilliant and punch the air and sing songs of heroism and happiness. All I felt was guilt. It wasn't the Baby Season's fault. *She* had forced it to chase us, and now I'd gone and put it back underwater. Well, I wasn't sorry I'd saved *us*, but I was sorry for *it*. And I was mad at her for making me do it.

"Come on," I said. "Mum and Dad will have our guts for garters."

And that's when Mum and Dad appeared through the hedge and hurried us back to the house across the road. I knew I was in trouble. But there are some kinds of trouble it's better to be in than others. I babbled about warning Neil not to go to AtmoLab, but nobody knew what Atmo-Lab was.

The two old hags were sitting on the wall. They looked even younger now, more Mum's age. Their hair seemed to be shrinking back into their heads, and their faces were unlined and their clothes shimmered with silver and lace. One of them clapped her hands delightedly; the other looked sideways down at us and winked.

"Thank you, dear, for saving our troublesome cat. We would have missed it if she'd taken it away from us."

"Catnapping," said the other. "Nasty sister."

"Yes, dear," the first said. "But not as nasty as us."

Then we all stopped and turned and looked down the road, listening to the sound of an engine getting louder and closer.

PART 3

The Maloneys and
the Míthráthúlacht

CHAPTER 17

NEIL

The van that held but just ourselves had been white once, maybe. Probably. Now it was mostly just dirt, thick and gray from the roof to the wheels. It was small and had something written on the side I couldn't make out. When they opened the back and threw me in, I landed on a bed of newspapers and coffee cups and bottles and rusty tools. The men in colored sweaters and kilts climbed in after me, sat me up against the wall, slammed the doors shut, and off we went.

One of them drove, with another beside him in the passenger seat. I was in the back with the other three. It wasn't very clean. Neither were the men. They all smelled sour and smoky, dusty, and dirty. It was hard to breathe, and I was shaking, my clothes clammy as ice against my skin.

One of the big men had a beard. The beard was thick

and had food and twigs in it. One was completely bald. His head looked like a piece of polished wood. The other had a spider tattooed on his face. I only realized it was a tattoo when he reached up and scratched his cheek. At first I thought it was a pet. Their woolen sweaters hadn't seen the inside of a washing machine in a long time. The sleeves were ragged and frayed, so that colored threads hung from their wrists, waving and twisting whenever they moved their hands about, and they moved their hands about a lot. They rolled some cigarettes with pieces of paper they filled with tobacco from pouches. They passed them round, and the acrid smoke covered the sour stink of the men and the van just a little.

"Boys!" Beardie said, looking down at me. "Would ye look at the state of him?" Then to me, "What the heck is wrong with ye, like?"

"What?" said Baldie. "What are ye on about, by?"

"Hypothermia, by! And shock, like. He's in a bad way!"

Baldie took a closer look at me. "Hey, boys, he's right, like. We're losing him, by."

"What's the matter, by?" Spidey said. "He's just a bit tired, like, aren't ye? Aren't ye?"

Spidey nudged me with an elbow. I tipped over into the back of the passenger seat. "Uh-oh," he said.

"Look at the old lips, like!" Beardie. "They're, like, totally purple!"

"Flip!" said Baldie. "The poor child, like! He'll waste away from the chills!"

"Get off them blankets there, by," said Spidey. "There you go, by. Wrap those around yourself."

A thick, heavy blanket that gave off clouds of dust and ash was dropped on me. It was warm, but I couldn't breathe. I was being polluted to death, which, when I thought about it later, turned out to be pretty ironic.

The blanket helped, but not much. I was exhausted. Rocked by the movement of the van, I was sinking away from the aching cold and into a deep, warm, dangerous sleep.

"AS I WAS GOIN' OVER THE CORK AND KERRY MOUNTAINS!"

The five voices boomed in the tiny space.

"I MET WITH CAPTAIN FARRELL AND HIS MONEY HE WAS COUNTIN'!"

My eyes opened and I gasped in shock.

"I FIRST PRODUCED MY PISTOL AND THEN PRO-DUCED MY RAPIER!"

I breathed in, filling my mouth and lungs with smoke, dust, ash, and the stink of the choirboys.

"I SAID STAND AND DELIVER OR THE DEVIL HE MAY TAKE YE!!"

I coughed and choked. Without missing a beat one of the singers gave me a heavy slap on the back.

"MISHU RIN DOR-RUM DO-RUM DO-RA!!"

I spat out a thin stream of water into my blanket. That was the closest it had come to being washed in a long time, though it was already damp through from my clothes.

"WHACK FOR THE DADDY-OH! WHACK FOR THE DADDY OH!!"

My head cleared a little. I began to shake off the warm sleepiness.

"THERE'S WHISKEY IN THE JAR-OH!!"

This lovely little song went on and on and on, and the singer was betrayed by his true love and flung in jail and was just plotting his escape when that song ended and they launched into another one, about a goat that got loose on Grand Parade, and after that yet another about a soldier's wife looking forward to her husband getting back from Salonika. I tugged the blanket up to my ears, but I couldn't keep the songs out.

By the time we got to wherever it was we were going I was tingling painfully all over.

The van turned and slowed and began to rock and bounce as though the road was made of nothing but rocks and holes. The lads stopped singing and they each put one hand on the floor and one hand on the ceiling and began to shout and whoop as though riding a rollercoaster. All my bruises and my bones and my muscles screamed with pain at each and every jerk and jolt. After an endless, agonising time the van finally stopped. I was crying silently.

The lads were amazed. They looked at each other and then at me. They tugged their beards and rubbed their bald heads, muttering to each other. They seemed to be feeling some guilt at the state of me, but not enough to do anything about it.

"We'll tell him, like," one of them said. "We'll tell him to hurry up."

"Needs a flippin' ambulance is what he needs, by!"

"Nah," one said and clapped me on the shoulder. I moaned, and he took his hand away as though it had been burnt. "Sorry, like, sorry, by! Come on lads, get a move on, like. We need to hurry."

They opened the doors of the van and helped me out. There was a fire smoking near some trees, and they sat me down next to it and blew on it until it flamed and fed it some wood. They told me to sit tight—"it would all be over soon, like, by,"—and then they ran off into the trees together, looking back over their shoulders as they went, as if they were abandoning a puppy in the snow.

I rubbed my hands and tried to warm myself by the fire, but I knew it wouldn't be enough. I had to get dry or I'd start losing fingers and toes.

I stood up and shook off the blanket. I pulled my T-shirt

over my head and kicked off my shoes. I nearly fell into the fire taking off my socks. Finally, I peeled my trousers down my numb legs. Shivering in my underwear, I enjoyed the prickly heat of the fire on my sodden skin for a while before picking up the blanket and rubbing myself dry. I turned around and let the warmth wash over my back. Wrapping my arms around myself, I took a look at my surroundings.

I was in a forest.

Brown and silver tree trunks were all around, and a gentle green rustle filled the air. Smoke from the fire drifted through the boughs and the slanting sunlight, rising up through a series of thick ropes that stretched between the trees above us. On the ground, mud and leaves and wood chippings all mixed in a thick soupy mess. Logs had been laid down, four wide, to make a path.

From what I could see, it looked like a large group of people had been living here for a while. Bags were everywhere. Black-and-white bin liners. Supermarket carrier bags. Green canvas bags. Rucksacks. Backpacks. The bags were full of rubbish or clothes or books or magazines or food or things that I couldn't identify and didn't want to. Large piles of sticks had been gathered here and there. Some turned out to be log piles, others turned out to be shelters. A guitar leaned against a tree near a sort of timber-framed kitchen. Plastic sheeting had been draped over it to keep out the wind and rain. Down the center, a long table was covered with fruit and vegetables, some half chopped or half eaten. There were pots and pans and lots of cutlery. Under the table there were freezer boxes of different shapes and sizes, and piles of posters and fliers with big, bold headlines like *SAVE THE TREES* and *STOP THE COUNCIL*.

I realized where I was.

Just outside Dublin, the local council had decided to chop down part of an old forest to make way for a motorway. A gang of eco-warriors had occupied the woods to protest against the development. They'd built tree houses and refused to move, delaying the works for well over a year. The whole thing had made national headlines. Any day now the forces of law and order were expected to come in and carry everyone off, and men with chainsaws were going to cut down all the trees.

Mum had had to practically tie me down to stop me from spending the summer up here in a tent, hugging the trees with the best of them.

"You don't know what sort of lunatic might be hanging around up there," she said. "You don't know what might happen to you!"

Maybe she'd been right.

As usual.

I walked across the clearing, my feet sinking into the mud. Twigs and thorns pinched my heels, but I barely noticed them. While the air shivered my skin, I poked around in bags until I hit the jackpot. I found fleeces, hiking trousers, shirts, socks, rain jackets, even a few pairs of waterproof boots. It took ages to dress, with the feeling coming painfully back into my hands and feet giving me pins and needles, but soon I was wearing a set of warm dry clothes and socks and boots, all too large for me. I didn't care.

I went into the timber-framed kitchen and grabbed apples and bananas and bread and ham and butter and jam. I fiddled with a little gas stove until I got it working and put on a kettle to make some tea. I took it all back to the fire and sat and ate. I cupped my hands around the mug and drank the hot tea, warming up bit by bit.

Somewhere nearby, out in the trees, something rattled. I looked up, but could see nothing. There were more noises. Booms. Shouts. Undergrowth crackling. Shouting. Screams. They seemed to be all around me, closing in.

Breathing hard, I listened as the sounds grew louder and closer. The boomings and the rattlings were drums. The forest was full of people playing drums and running around screaming and shouting. Well, for all I cared, they could trip and fall and break their necks. I held my mug in my hands and stayed sitting.

Something bright and shiny and fast swept into the clearing. I saw teeth and claws and feathers. I tried to follow it as it tore through the clearing and back into the trees, when another one rushed in from the other side and straight at my head. I made a sort of thin, high-pitched *eeeee* sound as it looped around me and around me and around me. The *eeeee* went on for a very long time, even after the thing flung itself upward and vanished in the high branches of the trees.

The clearing was full of them. I couldn't count them because they were moving too fast and anyway I didn't really care how many of them there were, even one was too many. They gave off a glow like bottled moonlight, but they weren't made of light: they were animals and birds, all smooth and streamlined and fitted out with jet engines. Bear snouts, wolf jaws, eagle beaks, badger claws . . .

I squeezed my eyes shut. *You're asleep,* I told myself. *You are having a dream. You think it's a nightmare, but it's not. All these wonderful animals have come to play with you and be your friends.* But when I opened my eyes again, they were still there, and they did not look friendly.

Then they slowed in their weaving, sinuous dance and drifted gracefully into a ring, surrounding me and the fire, where they came to a stop. Each one drifted down to the ground and settled on the floor of the clearing. The glow faded, and I saw . . .

What did I see? One moment they were a superteam of flying things and the next they were all just people, standing on tall thin legs. Their claws and their wings and their hides and their feathers were costumes, and their beaks and jaws and insect eyes were masks. Nobody moved and nobody spoke. One by one they seemed to kneel, and as their knees reached the ground they jumped, and their legs split in half, and the top half gave a little skip, and the claws and the wings reached up and removed the heads, and under the heads were people who had been standing on stilts.

They were all breathing heavily, grinning and looking at me. They all went down on one knee, laid their masks and claws and stilts on the ground and bowed their heads.

"HAIL, SON OF THE WEATHERMAN!" they roared. I jumped.

"Uh, hi," I said. "Hail, you guys."

The one with the eagle mask stood and stepped forward. He had long dark hair and no beard and a pointy face with no tattoos.

"Hail, son of the Weatherman!" he bellowed at the top of his voice, as if I were deaf or a long way away or there was a jet plane taking off beside us. "Well met indeed!"

He swept his hand back and around, taking in the crowd of weirdos. "We are your Shieldsmen! We have returned in this, your darkest hour, to do our duty and deliver you from your foes!"

"Oh," I said. I blinked and tried to think. I'd done it. I'd found them. Or they'd found me. I had gotten myself found by them. Yeah, that sounded OK. I felt as though I were floating, buoyed up by sheer joy. It seemed important to say something good and right and impressive. "Er. You are?"

"Yes!" he said. "We are! And, boy, are we happy to see you! Aren't we happy? Show him how happy we are, guys!"

They sprang up and waved their masks in the air and cheered and clapped and jumped up and down and rushed in and clapped me on the back and shook my hand, all grinning, their eyes lit up with joy and excitement. I just tried not to get stabbed or stepped on.

The spokeslunatic stepped through the crowd, leaned down, and reached out with his hand. Numbly, I lifted my hand, and we shook.

"Hi, Neil. Great to finally meet you. I'm Weisz."

I stared at his smiling face. In his eyes, a friendly light seemed to dance a merry little jig.

I opened my mouth to make a few small complaints about being kidnapped and nearly freezing to death, then shut it again. Never mind about that now.

"You need to all come back with me," I told him. "The Autumn is sort of blocked, and the Summer is sort of stuck and there's a thing that might be a new Season and a woman with terrible magic powers being a pain in the neck and trying to take Dad's job and . . ."

185

Weisz held up his hand and made little calming movements. He was still smiling, trying to say something reasonable. I just wanted to hit him. I could hear myself babbling and I wasn't even sure I was speaking English anymore. Finally I had to stop to breathe in.

"Of course we'll come back with you, Neil. We're your father's loyal Shieldsmen. We'll do whatever you ask. But I also have things to say to you. Serious things—and you must listen and understand."

"OK," I said uncertainly.

"I want you to know what this means to us. After all these years, that it should be us, that *we* should be the ones summoned once more to do our sacred duty." His voice grew thick, and he stopped for a moment and wiped his eyes. "Excuse me, this is a special, special day for all of us."

"I thought," I started. "We thought you'd gone. That there were no Shieldsmen left. Like the magicians at the club. And how did you know you'd been summoned? I didn't mention any summonses."

"Hmph, the club," Weisz snorted derisively. "A bunch of doddering old men who barely knew what day it was, let alone what Season. They let themselves be destroyed by the modern world, bought and sold like so much meat. They weren't worthy. And now AtmoLab is even worse. We were watching their headquarters—that's how we knew where to find you. Back when the club was still a going concern, you see, we had some contact, and they kept us informed about the Weatherman and his family—sent us photographs and such. Only baby photographs of you, of course, but you look like your dad, and, anyway, as soon as you turned up, AtmoLab suddenly had its own tropical storm in the lobby, so who else would you be? What was that storm, anyway?"

"Uh, it was an elemental sent by a hag who's kidnapped the thing that might be a new Season."

Weisz whistled and shook his head in amazement. "Interesting times! Are there a lot of them about? Wouldn't mind finding out how we'd match up to one of those buggers, eh?"

"Well," I said, trying to imitate Dad, "the simple ones are everywhere, of course. That was a complex one they must have conjured up out of simple ones somehow. Er, you want to fight one?"

"Of course! That's what we're for! We are the warriors of *Dunphelim*! The sworn shields of the *Fear Na hAimsire*, and no *dúil* is going to threaten our Chief! This is the time of the *Míthráthúlacht,* and the Shieldsmen stand ready to defend!"

The Shieldsmen gave a mighty shout while I tried to do a mental translation. *Fear na hAimsire* was "Weatherman." *Dúil* was "element." And *Míthráthúlacht* basically meant "The Bad Time."

"As for the summons, well, you're here, aren't you? The son of the Weatherman, searching for his servants and companions of old! That can only mean one thing can't it?"

"Uh, yeah! Yeah! You can consider yourself summoned! Really! Just get 'em all together, pack 'em up and let's go go go!"

He grinned. A sigh of relief came from the watching Shieldsmen and a terrific tension went out of the air.

"I mean, is this all of you, is it?" I asked. "If we could just pile into a few vans and cars and things and hit the road that'd be great!"

Weisz stood up and walked over to me and put his arm around my shoulder.

"We're the chosen, Neil. The youngest, the fittest, the strongest. The Shieldsmen have endured their exile for centuries now, living as a tribe apart, taking in husbands and wives from outside to keep the line strong, but all utterly dedicated to our duty: protecting the Weatherman. Passed down from generation to generation are our code, our mission, our training, and our skills. We have lived in glens, in bogs, in woods, and old ruins and abandoned villages. We have spent our lives training, preparing, watching—"

"NOBODY MOVE!"

Nobody moved.

"I've come for Neil! Don't get in my way and nobody gets hurt!"

A hulking figure wearing a black ski mask entered the clearing. He had a sword, which he waved in the direction of the Shieldsmen.

"Ed!"

The figure with the sword stopped threatening the Shieldsmen, who did not seem particularly threatened. His shoulders slumped. "I'm in disguise, Neil," he told me testily. "You're not supposed to use my real name."

"Ed!" I said. "It's OK! These are the Shieldsmen. They're on our side! I've summoned them!"

Ed swung his sword around on the Shieldsmen. "The Shieldsmen, huh?" He let his sword drop. "Well, all right. If Neil says you're OK, I suppose I'll let you off."

"How did you find me?" I asked.

"Well," he said, leaning on the sword. "The more I thought about it, the more I realized that this was the biggest gathering of people wearing the sort of clothes the people who took you were wearing. I'd nowhere else to look, so I chanced my arm. Good, eh?"

"Genius," I said.

"Also they had *Save the Trees* spray-painted on the side of the van."

"Aha!"

"And they'd been handing out leaflets along the canal."

"Oh."

"They even had a little map on them."

"Right."

"And they'd put up great big billboards along the road."

"Yeah."

"And I opened up today's paper and they'd done a big photo story on the protest and there they were, hanging out of a tree."

"OK, Ed."

"It was like the universe was trying to tell me something. Weird, huh?"

"Very! Can we go now?" I asked. "This is great and all, but we really need to get back home with the Shieldsmen so they can help Dad."

"Oh, yeah," Ed said. He took off his mask and looked around for somewhere to put the sword.

"After you went off with your new friends, yer man Holland came climbing out through that broken window looking fit to burst," Ed told me. "He wouldn't even let them other lads dry themselves! He just hustled them off to those two big black cars. Wherever they were going, they were in a tearing great hurry."

"Right," I said, and stopped. He was giving me a look. My sense of urgency got even *urgencier*. "Wait. You don't think they're going home, do you? To *my* home? Oh my God, come on, let's go!"

"No rush," he said airily, waving a hand. "We'll never catch 'em now, and, anyway, they're harmless."

"Harmless?"

"Mostly harmless. Besides, we can't go anywhere yet."

"What do you mean?" I asked. "Why can't we go any-where?"

"Because they've blocked the road. I had to park half a mile back and sneak up through the trees."

Everybody stopped talking.

"Who," asked Weisz carefully, "has blocked the road?"

"The police," Ed said. "Lots of them, and lots of men who aren't police. And they have trucks and backhoes, and trac-tors and trailers and things."

Twelve Celtic warriors all looked around uncomfortably.

"Um," one of them said, "they can't do this now! We're not in our eco-warrior disguises!"

"I probably should have mentioned that sooner," Ed said to me with a wince. "But I'd been thinking these were bad guys and that the police'd be a good distraction. Sorry."

"So what do we do now?" someone asked Weisz. "Are we going with Neil or are we protecting the trees?"

Weisz blinked, then looked at me.

Suddenly the world felt very heavy.

If I commanded the Shieldsmen to defend the forest they would. They'd climb up into their tree houses and the protest could go on practically forever. These guys would never give up. And I would want to climb right up there with them. But Dad needed them at the Weatherbox to fight a bigger battle. So I had to tell them to let the trees be destroyed and come with me to fight the Fitzgeralds. It's what they wanted, to be proper Shieldsmen again, but how much would they hate me for ordering them to walk away from the trees? This was so unfair. Weisz shouldn't be putting this on me.

Except he had to, didn't he? I was the son of the Weatherman. This was my job. If we didn't let these trees fall then a storm would come that would make all the trees fall.

"I'm sorry," I said. "Leave the trees. We have to go home."

They all bowed their heads, but they all straightened their backs and lifted their shoulders, too.

"Right," Weisz said, waving at the weapons. "Better put the cutlery away before the cops get here. Remember, we're leaving, not staying and fighting or protesting, so don't engage, avoid!"

Too late.

Police in fluorescent yellow jackets and workmen in bright orange overalls came marching grimly up the track. The lead policeman spotted the Shieldsmen, pointed, gave a shout, and they all broke into a run.

The police and the workmen streamed into the camp, the police charging straight for the Shieldsmen and—incidentally—me, the workmen making for the camp and the kitchen. In seconds there were struggling bodies all around me. Police hauled Shieldsmen away, and there was a dreadful babble of screaming and shouting.

I held my hands up and my palms out in the universal sign of *Please don't beat me up I'm harmless.* The timber frame of the kitchen crashed down. Bags and equipment and belongings were flung in a heap. A policeman went past with an armful of masks. A workman aimed a punch at a kneeling Shieldsman. I ran at him with both hands outstretched and shoved him into a tree. He sank down between the roots, staring at me with wide eyes. Four policemen closed in around me, and I was swallowed up in fluorescent yellow, while somewhere in the trees I could hear the chainsaws start to roar.

CHAPTER 18

LIZ

We knew straight away it was the wrong kind of engine. It didn't sound anything like Ed's truck at all.

Two huge black cars drove up and parked along the wall. They were bigger than some caravans I've seen. Doors opened with quiet, soft hissing noises, and three men and a woman got out. The car trunks opened like garage doors. I thought maybe a few smaller cars were going to drive out of the back of them, but the people began pulling out bags and boxes and stuff with wires attached, and a man stepped through the gate and walked up to us. The hags appeared, sitting on the wall, swaying gently. The people from the cars looked at them, then at each other, and carried on doing whatever it was they were doing.

"How are ye?" the man said. "Remember me?"

"No," Dad said. "Wait. You're . . ."

"Yeah. I am."

"Tony? What are you doing here? I thought you . . . What is all this?"

"Tony?" Mum said. "As in Tony *Holland*?"

"Yeah," the man said. "And that's Clive, Bob, and Cherie, there."

The three people looked up and gave little waves when he said their names.

"They'll be doing all the work. Heard of me, have you?"

"Nothing good," she said. "But I'd assumed it was lies."

"All true," he said. He didn't look very happy about it. He sighed and shrugged his shoulders. "Sorry. I'm the bad guy. I told the lies about your husband, I stole the money, and now I own all this. I have the deeds to the house, the rights to the phone box, the whole shebang. We'd have been down earlier like she wanted only we had a spot of bother, as the man says. Look, I've been over all this with that lad of yours, OK? Let's not have a fuss."

The two hags were dancing on the cars, quick little jigs, their bare feet darting up and down on the black metal.

"She," I said. "You mean Mrs. Fitzgerald."

He flinched.

"Neil?" Dad said. "You spoke to Neil? Do you know where he is?"

"Look, Maloney," Tony Holland said, like someone trying to be kind. "You can let us in and we can talk, or I can come back with a small army of lawyers and an eviction notice. It's up to you. The sooner we can get set up, the sooner we can solve this little problem of yours."

"The Autumn is late," Dad said through gritted teeth. "That's *not* a LITTLE problem!"

"WHERE'S MY SON?" yelled Mum, and threw herself at Tony Holland. Dad grabbed Mum and held her back.

"Your son? That vandal? He destroyed the AtmoLab headquarters! Flooded the whole place!"

"He did no such thing," Mum said in a low, dangerous tone.

"It's true! He left my office and went mad! Tore the place to pieces! I've never seen anything like it. The insurance company wants to classify it as an act of God! Your son is a dangerous lunatic, and, if he's not here, then I have no idea where he is!"

"AtmoLab," I said. "They sent the elemental to AtmoLab, that's what Hugh said. Is Neil OK? Is he OK?"

"Aye, last we saw him," said Clive. "That were when the lad got taken off by them other lads—big blokes, wearing skirts, in a van. I still think we should have called the cops."

"Wait," Dad said. "WHAT?"

"An elemental," said Bob, a small bearded man carry-

196

ing a big roll of white cables. "That's what he called it, him and his friend."

"Keep out of this, you two," Tony said.

"Did you say *skirts*?" Dad asked.

"Oh my God," Mum said.

Bob was shaking his head. "It weren't the lad that caused the havoc, I keep telling you. It were the . . . elemental thing."

"Freakish weather conditions," said Clive. "A random outbreak of freakish weather conditions. Never seen anything like it."

"Clive!" snapped Tony.

"I am going to kill each and every one of you and it is going to hurt a lot," Mum said.

"No," Dad said to Mum. "It's OK! He's OK!"

"It was amazing!" said Cherie. "It was a total rush! There was wind and rain and waves and lightning and a big huge cloud all inside the freaking lobby! That kid couldn't have done that! We'd be dead if they hadn't broken that window and got us out!"

"Big lads in skirts?" Dad said with a laugh. "It's the Shieldsmen! The Shieldsmen found him!"

"Are you sure?" Mum demanded. "How can you be sure?"

"Who else could it be? I'll bet anything they were watching the offices and saw him come out. It wasn't a kidnapping, it was a rescue!" Dad exclaimed.

I felt my heart beat faster. Was he right? Could it be true? It would be just like Neil to blunder around until the people he was looking for found *him*.

"None of that matters now," Tony said sadly. "Look, I hate to do this, but I'm doing it anyway because I have to. Step aside or I will call the police. Anyway, I thought this place was a guesthouse of some sort and we need to stay. Doing well enough to turn away paying guests, are you?"

"I'd turn you away any day of the week," Mum said.

The two hags were gone from the cars. I hadn't seen them go.

Dad held up a hand. "What do you mean? And what did you mean when you said about solving our problem? *How* are you going to solve it?"

"We'll fix it."

"Fix it? Fix it how?"

"Easy. We'll reconnect the phone line."

"You'll—you'll *what*?"

"You see the old line was badly out of date and in need of upgrading, so we had it remotely disconnected. Now we're going to go down and put in a new cable—brand shiny new and full of megabits and gigabots and whatever. It'll increase the speed of your Seasonal adjustment by a factor of up to a hundred!"

"YOU DISCONNECTED THE LINE?" Dad screamed.

"Can't upgrade without turning it off, can we?"

Dad stuck his finger right up under Tony Holland's nose. "You," he said. "You reconnect that line and you reconnect it *right now*! Do you have any idea what you've done? Do you have any idea what you're risking?"

Tony made a face.

"Some. More than you do, I expect. Tell you what. Let us in and get set up and we'll see what we can do, all right? The lads are keen to measure stuff and record stuff and they need to plug their gizmos in somewhere."

Dad withdrew the finger and made a fist, which shook with rage. His whole body seemed to tremble and shake like an ash tree on a windy day. His eyes changed. They went red and green, and his face seemed to become hollow and empty, and it twitched and a hundred long thin moving things like ivy branches spread across his cheeks and his forehead and his fist. Holland stared at him, frozen, eyes bugging out. I heard the creaking of old roots as they dragged themselves out of the ground.

Then Dad opened his fist and let his hand drop to his side. The lines were gone, his eyes were blue again, and the noise had stopped. He turned his back on Tony Holland and stalked into the house, and Tony Holland leaned against Clive and wiped sweat from his face, which had gone the same shade of yellow as the sky.

"That was awesome," said the girl quietly.

The AtmoLab crew came in and made themselves at

home. They went up the stairs with their bags and baggage and picked out rooms for themselves. After dropping their bags on their beds they went back out and finished unloading the huge cars, and then the huge cars were driven away. The windows were all dark and I couldn't see any drivers, so I assumed they were sort of robot cars that drove themselves. Clive, Bob, and the girl, whose name was Cherie, began unpacking their equipment out beside the phone box and running extension cables into the house, where they used every plug they could find.

Mum and Dad watched it all, helpless and unhelpful. Dad was bristling, Mum looked like all the cigarettes in the world would never calm her down or stop her from murderizing the next person who said a word to her, and me and Owen were standing there, the way you do when your mum and your dad can't do anything to stop the bad stuff from happening.

The phone in the house rang. Dad ran in and snatched it up. I held my breath, and Mum stood beside him with her hands on her hips, staring at him. Dad listened, nodded once, put the phone down, then turned to us with a sad, lost look on his face—and then the sad, lost look was gone and he was turning angry and red and his eyes were becoming big and deep and green.

He came out to the doorway and took hold of the jamb. Green leaves and brown vines flowed over and through his hands and into the wood of the door frame. He was nearly doubled over, as if his stomach hurt.

"I have to go to Neil," he said. "But I can't leave you."

Mum reached for him, but he waved her off. I could hear flies buzzing. A bumblebee flew out of his hair, which was longer, shaggier, stiffer.

"That was Ed. Neil and the Shieldsmen have all been arrested and taken to a police station."

"Dad?" I said.

"Twiggy Man," Owen said.

"I don't know what to do," he murmured, his voice a whisper like a breeze through a meadow of golden flowers.

"You should go," said one of the hags. They floated like pale gray ghosts in the hallway behind Dad. I could barely see their faces in the shadows over his shoulders. "Get that silly boy of yours back before he makes more of a mess."

"Never knew a family like it for messes," said the other.

"I can't leave them," Dad said. "I can't leave it—the Weatherbox."

"We'll mind it for you, dear. And them," the first hag reassured him.

"Quite good at minding things, us."

"We could mind it for a thousand years."

"But you'll want to be back quicker than that."

"Those tricksies with their electrics and their boxes full

of colors and their phoney roots will have the bell ringing long before midnight. You must be back, son and all, when the bell rings."

"Why would you help us? I asked them. "You're her sisters."

The hags looked at me.

"Oh, my little sweetie, not all families are like yours."

"She abandoned us. Deserted us."

"Grew young again."

"You're young again," said Owen.

"We are. And as we get younger, we get less crazy. We forget the things we knew. Knowing too much makes you crazy, you know, dear."

"But, you see, she's the eldest. When we're finished getting young again, we'll be the age we were when they made us serve the Black Pool, but that'll be no older than you and your sister, and no more powerful."

"She was supposed to be the witch, you see. They took her and trained her and taught her, not us."

"But they needed three sisters to stir and sing for the beast of the black hole, because they thought it was in love with the threefold goddess."

"They took us from our home and threw us in that shell and left us there for a thousand years. By the hokey, I wouldn't so much as sing for my supper or stir my own tea in the cup now for all the silk in China."

"You do a lot to pass the time for a thousand years. She taught us all she knew, but she was always the first, the eldest."

"The strongest."

"The smartest."

"We have time, before the bell rings, to keep her at a distance. And maybe, in the fight, later, we can do some good."

"And if we win, we'll send her back and she can stir and sing by her lonesome."

"And if the black beast don't like it he can go boil himself in a kettle and call himself soup."

"Your names?" Mum asked.

"Hazel, they called me."

"My name is Ash."

Mum and Dad looked at each other.

Mum nodded. "Go and get Neil," she said.

"Stand back," he told us, and we stood back, and he turned into something else—something big and covered in leaves and twigs and branches and full of living creatures. There was a smell of things growing and rotting, and I heard insects and birds. A fox barked, and Dad had long trailing vines for hair and his hands were covered with tree bark and his face was all wrong, lumpy, and swollen, like a ripe fruit ready to burst.

"Do not let them touch that line," he said, and then he

203

was gone, and there was mud everywhere and flies and worms and the rich smell of high summer.

"Twiggy man!" I said.

Mum put her hand to her mouth. "Oh my God."

The two hags came through the doorway, younger than ever—their skin smooth, their hair black, their faces sharp.

"The Weatherman in his might goes boldly to the place of his son's imprisonment," said Ash. "Green his strength, bright his rage. His shield is the earth. His sword is fire. His spear is of water, and his chariot the air. All empty is the land from his passing."

"I thought you said you'd do no more of that singing," said Hazel.

"That wasn't singing, you *oinseach*, that was chanting, all solemn and proper for the occasion."

I looked at the AtmoLab people working around the Weatherbox.

"Will Dad be back in time?" I asked.

"Oh, good heavens, dear, don't worry your little head about that," said Ash. "Of course he won't."

"Not a hope in the world," agreed Hazel.

"Right," I said.

I went to buy more time for the Weatherman—which meant keeping AtmoLab away from the Weatherbox.

CHAPTER 19

NEIL

I was quite thoroughly and repeatedly arrested.

"I didn't do anything," I said as I was led down a logging path to the main road, where cars and fire engines, ambulances, and bulldozers, backhoes, and tractors stretched along the verge for a mile in either direction. Eco-warriors and Shieldsmen were being put into white vans. I saw Weisz, his face pale with shock. One of the other Shieldsmen looked over at me and gave a shrug.

Then people in suits and uniforms surrounded me and started fighting over me. The police wanted to stick me in the paddy wagon. The guys from the ambulance wanted to put an oxygen mask on me. The firefighters wanted to put me over their shoulders and carry me to safety. There was a reporter who kept yelling questions at me. There was a man from the county council who screamed and shook his fist at me.

The blue lights of the police cars flashed and turned. Bulldozers and tractors roared and rattled. The buzz of chainsaws and the crash of falling wood came from the forest. One of the eco-warriors was weeping, resting his head on the shoulder of a burly policeman, who was patting him awkwardly on the back.

After being swung this way and that a few times they finally tossed me into the back of the paddy wagon. I sat on the bench next to the door. Weisz was beside me, and there was a line of slumped and tired-looking Shieldsmen sitting on either side, their knees all sticking out and meeting in the middle.

"Full up!" a policeman yelled, and the doors slammed shut and a fist pounded on them and we all rocked and rolled as the paddy wagon pulled out.

"That's an awful pity, by," someone said. "They were nice old trees, they were. And what's the point, like? There's no money left in this country, so they'll cut them down, like, and sell the wood and all the profit will go into some politician's pocket, and then they'll tear the place up for a while and dig a few holes and pour a bit of concrete and then, like, all the finance will run out and it'll be left like that, a wreck and a ruin."

"They'll widen the road," someone else said, bitterly.

"Great, by. Nice wide roads and no one left to drive on them because no one can afford a car."

"Forget that," Weisz said, loudly. "That's not important anymore. The son of the Weatherman is present and we have been called. Remember your duty."

"Are we all going to jail?" I said. "I don't want to go to jail. How can you do your duty in jail?"

"Don't worry," Weisz replied. "They'll charge us, stick us in the cells, and a judge will set bail and we'll be out by lunchtime tomorrow."

"Tomorrow? God, Weisz, we don't have that much time! You don't understand how urgent this is!" I snapped.

I spent the rest of the journey trying to explain how urgent this was. I ended up yelling at them.

"We've got to escape and get home and protect my family from *her*! We've got to get the phone line fixed so the Seasons can change! You're magic Celtic ninja warriors! Surely you can escape from a paddy wagon!"

The paddy wagon stopped. The doors swung open. We blinked at the light and climbed down onto a footpath in front of a police station.

"Now's your chance!" I hissed at Weisz, but he just smiled vaguely and shuffled his feet.

I gave up and turned to one of the policemen. "Uh, excuse me, where's Ed? My friend, Ed Wharton? Big guy. He had a sword."

"Him and everyone else! But if you mean the big guy with the sword but no kilt, we let him go. Turns out your Mr. Wharton had a permit. Never saw a permit for a sword before, but there you go. Gave him a warning and told him to get out of Dublin. None of the rest of you had permits, though. What were youse doing, anyway? One of those arty street-parade things? We loved the costumes, by the way. Excellent craftsmanship! Let us know if you're doing a festival, will you? We all want to come along and see you in action."

Inside the station it was bedlam. There was a mob of shouting, singing eco-warriors, a smaller mob of eco-warrior lawyers, reporters, councilors, and a few workmen and, trying to manage it all, the policemen in their peaked caps and yellow jackets. The Shieldsmen were put sitting in a row on a bench where they started singing some sort of sad and soulful harmony, which was actually quite lovely and everyone quieted down to listen. Someone tried to ruin it by strumming along with a guitar, but a policewoman confiscated it as evidence. When they finished, the whole station applauded, and then got back to the outrage and anger and everybody trying to make themselves heard at once.

The walls were covered with official posters telling me all about the various laws and acts and regulations I might be breaking just by being alive. One of the Shieldsmen was tearing them down and stuffing them into the pockets of her kilt.

Then I was taken by the elbow and led sideways through the mob, up to a tall desk where a massive sergeant was looking out over the whole scene with an air of patient, long-suffering gloom. He was trying to take down the details of an excited eco-warrior who seemed to think he was there to file a complaint about police brutality instead of be arrested.

"Evening, Sarge!" said the policeman. "Keeping you busy?"

"Well," he said slowly and thoughtfully. "If they weren't I'm sure you will."

"Just boost this one through for us, Sarge," the policeman said. "Then we'll be out of your hair."

Sarge sat back in his chair, making the plastic creak and crack. He pointed a big meaty finger at me. "This one, is it?"

"That's the one, Sarge."

"That's the one," Sarge repeated. "What's he done, may I ask? Murder? Terrorism? Serial killing? Must be a dangerous brute, whoever he is. What are we dealing with here, exactly?"

"Knocked someone over," the policeman said. "Nearly crippled him."

"I'm sorry," I wailed. "I didn't mean to! It was an accident!"

"I see," said the sergeant, looking directly at me. "You look like the crippling sort, all right. Name?"

"Excuse me!"

Everything fell quiet. The singing and the talking and the shouting and complaining all died down. The air glowed strangely, and the evening sun shone green and gold through the windows. Thick clouds of pollen were flowing through the shafts of light.

Sarge looked up, blinking, eyes streaming. He sniffled and pulled out a handkerchief. "It's a bit late in the year for hay fever," he muttered.

"I want you to let him go."

"Dad?" I said.

A space had cleared behind us, where everyone had pressed back and away from the man standing there—Dad, but different. There was something green about him, something dark, and there was a smell—or a hundred different smells—of plants and dirt and manure and rain on hot dust. In the quiet of the police station, I could hear a buzzing noise, rising.

"And who are you?" demanded Sarge.

"I'm his father," Dad said. "I'm the Weatherman. *Is mise Fear Na hAimsire*, and I've come for my son."

A murmur ran through the crowd. I saw men and

women in bright woolen jumpers push forward, eyes alight.

Weisz stepped out. "Weatherman," he said.

"Shut up," Dad said. "I'm here for Neil. I'm taking him now. Don't try to stop us."

Sarge sat back in his chair and studied Dad. "Is that right? I see. Well, of course. He's only under arrest for assault. We're only the police. It's only our job to enforce the law of the land. By all means, off you go."

He waved his hands, then held up a finger as if he'd just had an idea.

"Or, no," Sarge said. "Here's a better notion. You sit yourself down. You shut yourself up, and you let us do our job. How does that sound?"

"No," Dad said. "We're leaving."

"OK," said Sarge. "Lads?"

A policeman took hold of my arm. Other policemen pushed past the Shieldsmen, reaching for Dad. The Shieldsmen blocked them and tried to pull them back. The policemen turned on the Shieldsmen. Voices were raised. So were fists.

"STOP!"

Dad was taller now, almost to the ceiling, and his skin was green and his clothes were made of leaves, and his hair was grass and his body was wrapped in ivy and briars and brambles. Behind him the doors of the police station blew open and a million flying, buzzing, whirring insects flew in.

That's when the screaming really started.

Summer hits like a hammer. It's great after a long Winter and a wild Spring, when everything gets bright and hot and flowers burst and insects buzz and birds dart and fruit ripens, but it is life pushed as far as it can go.

Summer exploded into the police station. A billion insects surfed a blaze of heat and light. Thick dark soil boiled up from the ground under our feet, squirming with centipedes and worms. Trees ignited from cracks in the walls and ceiling, sending out long crooked branches thick with leaves and heavy with fruit that swelled and ripened and died and rotted and fell about us in a couple of seconds. The stench of rot and earth and mad growth would have driven us crazy if we weren't already insane with buzzing, biting, crawling insects.

On my skin and up my nose, in my mouth, my ears, my clothes. Crawling, touching, buzzing, biting in my hair and all over me, alive, fat, hungry, and thirsty. They were IN MY EYES!

Then I was yanked off my feet, lifted by a giant hand that went around my waist and carried me through the nightmare. People screamed and yelled and prayed and wept and ran around looking for the doors. I was taken through it all and set down outside. I saw nothing because

I had my eyes shut tight. I shook myself hard and slapped myself and my hair to get the insects off, and finally I opened my eyes. Inside the station there was golden light and black insects and green growing things and running, falling people clawing their way outside.

I was standing in the car park. There were people all around—eco-warriors and Shieldsmen and police and detectives and criminals, all coughing and rolling and wiping themselves and hugging and weeping and staring, and all keeping well clear of the man standing beside me, fear in their eyes and horror on their faces.

"Dad," I said.

"It's OK, Neil. I've come to take you home."

He wasn't all summery now, though there was still a kind of glow around him—a green tinge to his skin and a dark red in the depths of his eyes. He seemed more sad than anything else.

Ed ran up, red-faced and puffing. "Neil? Neil, are you OK?"

"Hey, Ed. I'm OK. I just feel, you know, like there's still insects all over me."

"Uh, there are. Here, let me . . ."

"Agh! Agh! Get 'em off! Get 'em off!" I yelled.

"Stop struggling!"

"Ow! Stop hitting me!"

"Sorry!" Ed said. "They're really dug in there!"

213

"Agh!"

"Still, wow, did you see that? Did you see it? Wow! I didn't know your dad could do that!"

"Neither did I!"

"I'm glad I wasn't in there, though. I followed you here and rang your dad. Didn't expect him to get here so quick."

"Is that it? Is that all of them?"

"All the big ones anyway. The smaller ones should wash off in the shower."

"OK, Ed," Dad said. "Take us home."

"OK. Uh, couldn't you just, y'know . . ." He wiggled his fingers in the air.

"I'm not sure I could bring you with me. Alive, anyway. I sent Neil off on his own and now I'm going to make very sure he gets back safely. How long is the drive?"

"Two hours, give or take," Ed replied.

"That's too long. Could you manage it in an hour and a half?"

"Uh, well . . ."

"Go as fast as you like. No one," he said, "is going to stop us."

"It *is* a racing truck," I reminded Ed.

"OK," Ed said. "Yeah. I can do that."

"Come on then," Dad said.

"Dad, wait!" I cried.

"What? Why?" he asked.

214

"Dad, I found them. I found the Shieldsmen! They're the people in the woolly sweaters. You have to bring them with us! They've been waiting so long, and we need them!"

Dad looked around at the ring of men and women in dirty sweaters who had gathered to stand sheepishly in a half circle before him.

Weisz came forward with his head bowed and his arms by his side. "Weatherman," he said. "We stand ready to serve."

"Shieldsmen," Dad said. "Did you serve my son by allowing him to be arrested?"

The Shieldsmen bowed their heads even further in shame. I opened my mouth to defend them, but stopped. I guess it was Dad's call, in the end.

"Still," he said. "We all make mistakes. There is a great joy in me to call your exile ended. Come back with me now and guard my fort once more."

Weisz's face lit up with joy. The Shieldsmen grinned and thumped each other's shoulders.

"We'll never fit that lot in the truck," Ed said.

"You," Dad said, pointing at a policeman sitting on the ground with his legs splayed, pulling ivy out of his hair.

"Yes?" he said. "Oh, no, please leave me alone. I'll be good! I'm sorry we arrested him, I really am!"

"Get me the keys to one of those vans," Dad told him.

The policeman scrambled to his feet and ran off. He

came back about a minute later and held a set of keys out to Dad. They jangled as his hands shook. "It's OK. You don't have to bring it back. We'll say it was stolen. It's the van that all the masks and things were put in. Please don't come back."

"I won't," Dad said. "Thank you."

"Er, when can we have our police station back?"

Dad shook his head. "I'm sorry. It's not your police station anymore."

The last few people had run or crawled outside. Grass and earth and trees and water were all squeezing out through the doors and windows now. Crashing noises came from inside as the floors collapsed. Then the roof caved in, and a great halo of insects swooped out and around. Green shoots burst upward.

Dad gave the keys to the Shieldsmen, who went looking for the van. We followed Ed to where he'd left the truck.

"We'd better make a bit of haste," Ed said. "I think you just declared war on the police."

"They declared war on me first," Dad said. "And they lost."

CHAPTER 20

LIZ

I had my bow in my hand, arrows in my belt, war paint on my face, and crow feathers in my hair. The heat was sticky, and the sky was bright, even though the sun had gone down. I was standing on the phone box and I was pointing an arrow at AtmoLab, hoping that I wouldn't have to find out whether I was mean enough to shoot at what seemed like a bunch of perfectly nice and friendly people. Mum was standing in front of the door of the phone box with her arms crossed and an expression on her face scarier than a hundred arrows. Owen and Neetch were chasing each other around and around the phone box and Mum's legs, laughing and jumping. Ash and Hazel stood side by side on the wall.

After Dad left, AtmoLab had carried on, attaching their computers to things that measured the wind, the humidity, the temperature, and a hundred other things that the computers calculated and processed and analyzed. They had pointed lights and cameras and sensors and detectors at the phone box. Clive had opened a small metal hatch on the road beside the phone box and pulled out a cluster of wires and cables, snipping and splicing and pulling and twisting and untangling.

They were reconnecting the phone line, and they seemed like perfectly lovely people, but they were the enemy and had to be stopped. Or at least they had to be stopped until Dad was ready for them. I had screamed my best Shieldsman battle cry at the top of my voice and charged and leaped over the wall and run around with my bow and arrow screaming and screaming like a crazy dangerous person until I had chased them all away. Then I climbed on top of the Weatherbox and told them that if any of them took one step nearer I'd skewer them.

"We're here to help," Clive said with a nice, friendly smile, waving his hands up and down.

"That's right, lass," Bob added. "Just let us in and we'll have this phone box back working in no time!"

"Shiny boxes and phoney roots," said Hazel.

"Blunt little knives," said Ash.

"Uh," said Bob. "They're called screwdrivers."

"Roots carry the signal," Hazel said. "Not the weather."

"The Weatherman is the Door," said Ash. "Not the box and not the lake."

"When is a Door not a Door?" asked Hazel.

"When is a Weatherman not a Weatherman?" added Ash.

"When is a Weatherman not a Door?" remarked Hazel.

"Oh God! Oh God, what are you doing? Get away from there! Get away now!" Tony Holland interrupted, running down the path and out through the gate. He tripped and stumbled to a stop in front of Mum.

"Look," he said. "Don't do this. You must have some idea what she's like. You must! You have to let them work!"

"No," Mum said. "We don't. Go away, all of you. Go away while you still can."

"Look," Tony said again, moving his arms and bobbing his body up and down like Owen when he's nervous or excited. He kept turning his head one way and another, looking up and down the road as if Mrs. Fitzgerald was going to come flying down on us any second now. "Listen, I'm begging you. Just let them reconnect the line and we'll be gone. I can put this behind me and forget this whole thing. My whole life has been on hold, you know? My whole life! Can you imagine? Can you imagine what it's like? Course you can't. You've no idea. None. I want my life back!"

"You don't really think she'll let you go, do you, Tony?"

Mum said, looking at him as if he were a dog that had just made a mess on the carpet.

"She promised!" he said. "She said once it was working again I could go home and she'd never bother me again! I want to go home! And you won't stop me!"

"I'm not stopping you, Tony. Go on. Go home, if you want."

"I can't! You don't know what she's like! You don't know what she can do—so shut up, right! Shut up and go away!"

"Don't talk to my mum like that, you rotten lying coward!" I shouted, nocking an arrow and drawing it back.

He stared up at me in disbelief. "Put that down before someone gets hurt, you stupid little—"

The arrow went past his head. He screamed in pain and clutched his ear. I felt a shock go through me. I hadn't actually meant to hit him. I ignored it and tried to look tough and mean, like a Shieldsman should.

Clive and Bob and Cherie were standing with eyes and mouths wide with shock.

"She'll kill me!" Tony screeched, hands over his ear and blood on his shirt. "She'll kill you, too! For God's sake! Ow!"

He took a step forward, but Mum got in front of him.

"Step back," she said. "Step back and go home, you great fool."

Now the three AtmoLabbers were moving to help their boss. I nocked another arrow. Neetch flowed down around the Weatherbox and grew, and all his hair stood up and he bared his teeth and hissed. They all took a step back then. Owen stood beside him and stroked his back.

"You're scaring him," he said. "You shouldn't scare him."

"Look," Bob said. "Nobody wants anyone to get hurt."

"We're just trying to help," Cherie said. "Look, Tony's bleeding. We have to call an ambulance."

"You don't know what you're doing," Mum said. "You don't know who you're working for and you don't know what it means. You should drop everything and walk away and not look back."

"GET BACK TO WORK!" screamed Tony. "Never mind them! Never mind me! Forget everything! Fix that line and fix it now or you're fired! You're all fired!"

"There are worse things than being fired," Mum said.

"Nothing else matters!" said Tony. He was pleading with everyone. "Don't be scared of them and don't be scared of me! Be scared of *her*! She's worse than anything you can imagine!"

"Who?" asked Clive.

"FIX IT!" screamed Tony.

That's when Mum pushed him. She put both hands on his chest and shoved him hard, and sent him sprawling back across the road.

"What the hell is wrong with you people?" said Clive. "Have you gone crazy? It's only a phone box!"

Neetch hissed again, raising an outstretched paw and long wicked claws.

"I don't think he likes you talking to us like that," Owen said.

Mum stood over Tony.

"Get out," she said. "Get far, far away from here."

She pointed at the AtmoLabbers, then pointed down the road. "Go."

"Go nowhere!" Tony roared from all fours. Clive and Bob helped him up and took him over to a spot on the wall, as far away from the Weatherbox as they could get, while Cherie found a first-aid kit and wiped the blood off Tony's ear. I thought I was going to throw up. I lowered the bow, and Neetch curled up on the ground and Owen nestled into him and fell asleep. Mum looked up at me and smiled, and I nodded back down at her because I couldn't quite remember how to smile just then. I squatted down, the bow and arrow held loose in my hands and we commenced to waiting.

Time passed, the sky grew dark, and the air turned cold. There was no wind, not even a breeze. I saw strange clouds rising on the horizon. On all the horizons. To the east, climbing over the mountains, glowing green and sinister; to the west, billowing like smoke, filled with a deep angry red; in the north, beyond the hill, spreading itself wide, a dark rolling purple. And in the south, behind our house,

222

there was a blank gray haze, as if the sky itself were vanishing bit by bit into nothingness.

"Here they come!" said Hazel.

"All the Seasons but one," agreed Ash.

"Three in the sky. One on the road."

"And the babby in his bath."

"Put that down, Liz," Mrs. Fitzgerald said, stepping out of the trees and crossing the road to stand beside the Weatherbox. "You don't need it anymore."

CHAPTER 21

NEIL

Ed drove like a lunatic. He swerved around cars, blew his horn at anyone going under eighty kilometers an hour, went the wrong way down one-way streets, drove on the wrong side of the road, and generally acted like a road hog. If he'd driven like this on the way up I'd have spent the trip under the dashboard. I felt sorry for the other drivers—and occasional pedestrians and cyclists. It must have been terrifying to have a ten-ton truck, driven by a one-ton maniac, bear down on you and then whip past. But mostly, I was looking at Dad.

You can't look at your dad the same way after he's unleashed a little pocket Summer in a police station. You can't look at anything the same, really, but particularly not your dad.

"Dad," I said. "That was amazing."

He looked at me, ran a hand through his hair, shook his head, and sighed. "No, it was stupid."

"But Dad, I—"

"Listen, Neil, what I just did was forbidden. Absolutely forbidden. It means I can't be the Weatherman anymore. I had to do it. I have to get you home as fast as possible, and I'd do it again, but I've played right into Mrs. Fitzgerald's hands. If they weren't going to fire me for the delay with the Weatherbox, they're definitely going to fire me for this. I'll be lucky if they don't do worse."

"Worse?" I knew the story of the Weatherman who'd destroyed the fort and banished the Shieldsmen and Weathermages. That couldn't happen to Dad. Could it?

"Never mind that now. I have to get you home. I have to get you home before the Seasons assemble over the Door to judge me and appoint a new Weatherman. It has to be you, because otherwise it's going to be her."

"But, Dad, she's too strong!"

Dad smiled. Even his teeth looked green. "I've become the Summer, Neil. I can't do it for long and I'm only supposed to do it in the direst of emergencies, and I'm going to pay for doing it. But I'm not finished yet."

"Oh. Wow! Dad, I . . . I . . ." I felt slightly ill. Whether it was from Ed's driving or from what Dad was saying, I wasn't sure. It didn't matter. Dad had become the Season. To rescue me. And now Dad couldn't be Weatherman

225

anymore. Because of me. And it was starting to look like I would never be Weatherman, either. Oh. My mouth was dry. My head felt light. I bent over in my seat because suddenly my stomach was cramping. Dad patted me gently on the back.

"What are we going to do?" I asked. My voice was muffled because my head was between my knees.

"I'm going to fight Mrs. Fitzgerald," Dad said. "You're going to become the Weatherman."

"I am?" I sat up. "Oh. Right. OK. Uh, Dad? I'm not ready to be the Weatherman. I'm really not."

"I'm not ready to stop being the Weatherman, but we don't have a choice."

"Sorry to interrupt," said Ed. By now we'd torn through the city and out onto the motorway, rolling down the outside lane with horn blaring and lights flashing. "I think you two should have a look outside. There seem to be unusual weather phenomena all over the place."

We looked out through the windscreen, then out the side windows and the back. The police van full of Shieldsmen was following on the road behind us. Weisz gave us an excited thumbs-up from the passenger seat.

Climbing into the sky from all points of the compass except the south were heavy masses of cloud, building fast and full of light—red, green, and purple—sweeping like an avalanche across the sky.

"That's them," Dad said. "Faster, Ed. Faster."

The needle on the speedometer jumped until it couldn't go any higher.

"Them?" I asked, scared now, of the speed and the clouds and the note in Dad's voice.

"The Seasons," Dad explained. "All except Summer, who is here already and who, for the moment, I have inside me."

"Wow," Ed said, turning on the radio. "Best holiday ever!"

"'Supercell thunderstorms are rare but not unknown,'" said a voice on the radio. "'You see, what happens is you get these giant columns of cloud that sort of pull up hot humid air in a powerful rotating updraft. You can expect heavy downbursts of rain and hail accompanied by thunder and lightning and possibly even tornadoes. Alarming, but explicable. What's slightly terrifying is that three of them have formed spontaneously out of nowhere and are now crossing the country from the east, west, and north, respectively, all looking to converge somewhere over the Midlands.'"

"'And in your considered scientific opinion, will that create a massive super-mega-terror storm that could lay waste to the entire country?'" asked someone else on the radio.

"'That's the optimistic outlook, yes. We should probably evacuate.'"

"'The Midlands?'"

"'The country.'"

"'And what if they are, in fact, alien mother ships disguised as clouds about to commence a devastating global invasion to enslave humanity?'"

Dad switched the radio off. "Listen carefully, both of you. We don't know what will be waiting for us when we get home, but Neil has to stay safe at all costs. Neil, whatever is there, whatever has happened, whatever you see, I want you to run for the lake as fast as you can. Take the Shieldsmen. They'll protect you."

"The lake? Oh God. OK. What about you?"

"I'll be fine. I'll keep Mrs. Fitzgerald occupied, but Hugh and the elementals will be after you."

"Hugh?"

"Run for the lake, you hear? Straight up through the woods to the lake."

"Why?"

"And Ed, listen, when we get there you're to do exactly as I say, you hear? Don't question me, just do it."

"Uh, OK," said Ed. We'd left the motorway now, and the truck leaned to one side as we went through a roundabout.

"There's something else, Neil. I've been thinking about the Gray Thing—the new Season."

"So you really think it is a fifth Season? Dad, how can that work? What's it the Season of? Where would it fit? What would we call it?"

"We don't have to call it anything yet. We just don't know yet what it's for or why they made it."

"Doesn't making another Season violate the agreement?" Ed said.

"It depends," Dad said. "Two things have occurred to me. One is that it may take centuries for the Baby Season to mature. The other is that we don't know whether Seasons die. We don't know whether in the past Seasons *have* died. And been replaced."

"You . . ." I said, and shook my head to try and get my thoughts to work properly. "You think that one of the big Seasons is dying and the Baby Season is going to take its place? And you think it's happened before?"

"Seems like the sort of thing you'd notice," Ed said.

"As far as I'm aware," Dad said, "No scientist has yet made a study of the life cycle of a Season. Anyway, that's just a theory."

"That's some theory, Dad," I said.

"Here's what I think happened," Dad said. "Mrs. Fitzgerald, the third hag, left the Black Pool and traveled south to the Midlands. She decided that the only way to be sure of not being sent back was to have another, even more important, job. She decided to become the Weatherman. First she tried to steal the gate, using John-Joe to swindle my father. Then, when the Weathermen's Club moved the Doorway, she set out to destroy the club, using Tony Holland. Tony wrecked the club's finances, bought it out, gained control of the phone line and, finally, this summer, cut the line off. And they did all this right under my flippin' nose! Make no mistake, I don't deserve to be Weatherman anymore."

"Dad, it wasn't your fault," I protested.

"It was, Neil, and that's all there is to it. I cut myself off from the club and let it be destroyed. That's on me. To protect the gate and the agreement—that's my job, Neil. I failed."

"Oh, Dad."

"It's OK. It's not over yet. Mrs. Fitzgerald must have sensed the presence of the Baby Season in the lake, but she waited—and when the time was right, she provoked it into creating all the anomalous weather until finally you went down and freed it. The young Weatherman freed the young Season. Then she captured it and now she's using it, even after Liz sunk it down into the bog—probably a bit like I'm using the Summer. It's young and vulnerable in a way the other Seasons aren't. And it allows her to control elementals, making her incredibly powerful and dangerous.

"With the Season late, I'm in disgrace. She knows the power I have, but she also knows I'm reluctant to use it. If I use it, I'm finished, which is what she wants, but I'm also every bit as dangerous and powerful as she is, so it's a risk. Once the Seasons were well and truly furious with me, her plan was to have the line reconnected. Her people are working on it right now, but I'd know if they'd finished. When the Autumn comes through, chances are I'll be deposed and she'll offer herself as a better candidate than you. She may use the Baby Season as a bargaining chip; I'm not sure. Now, though, I've used my power and the three Seasons are coming, and . . ." He trailed off.

"What?" I said. "What does that mean?"

"I don't know," he said. "Neither does she."

"But why do you want me to go to the lake, Dad? I don't understand!"

"How are we doing, Ed?" Dad asked.

"We'll be there in twenty minutes, give or take, so long as we don't hit anything."

"Don't stop," Dad said. "Don't slow down."

"Don't hit anything," I said.

Dad looked over at me. "It's you or her, Neil. So it has to be you."

He turned in his seat, put one hand on each of my shoulders, and leaned in close. "I know what it's like, Neil. I know what it's like to have everything you thought was safe and secure suddenly fall apart, and for someone to come in and take it all away from you. I know what it's like to watch your dad lose it all and to have the whole weight of the world come down on your shoulders. You're gentle, Neil, and I don't mean that as a bad thing. It's a good thing. The best. It's not something the rest of the world always values, but

I do. *We* do. You're a gentle young man, a real gentleman, and you've been through a lot, so you're strong as an ox, too, and you don't deserve to have all this fall on you. But I know you'll use your head and use your heart and get through it. I thought I was alone when my dad lost the farm, but it turned out I wasn't, and neither are you. We have our own little tribe, and when you're Weatherman you'll be the chief, so don't ever feel alone, or weak, or too scared to go on, OK? You're my son, and it's well pleased I am with you."

I nodded dumbly, and he put an arm around my head and pulled me to his chest, which smelled of rich green growing things. I breathed in deep and closed my eyes.

We drove on, tearing down the narrow country roads, horn blasting, right into the heart of the gathering storm. I thought of those old ghost stories about the man and his son on a horse-drawn carriage who, having vowed to race the storm home, were cursed to ride ahead of it forever. We didn't have forever. We had minutes. It got darker. It got colder. The sky was full of angry light.

Dad told me what had happened while I was gone, and I told him what had happened to me. Then we were quiet for a while. The roads grew familiar. My throat clutched, my heart jumped, my stomach clenched. I wasn't ready for any of this.

"There," Dad said. The old barn went past. Trees closed

around. It was as if we were falling down a dark tunnel, as if we were one of Liz's arrows in flight. There was the house, the Weatherbox, people clustered around it.

"Now," Dad said. Two white shapes flew from the roof of the Weatherbox.

Ed hit the beams. He sounded the horn. Faces turned in shock. Mum. Liz. Mrs. Fitzgerald. Three people I vaguely recognized rolled away from a hole in the ground. Hugh and John-Joe gaped from the ditch. Owen on the wall scooped up Neetch and jumped back onto the lawn. Mum, Liz, and Mrs. Fitzgerald scattered. I braced myself, and shut my eyes.

Under the rumble and the roar, as if echoing across hillsides and over treetops, I heard the far-off sound of a telephone ringing.

CHAPTER 22

LIZ

They were coming from the east, the west, and the north, blazing clouds blocking out the dead yellow sky. Huge and angry and ominous. The sky was filling up with Seasons, and we were running out of time.

Hugh, glowering, and John-Joe, grinning like an idiot, followed Mrs. Fitzgerald across the road like a pair of headless chickens. Hugh saw me up on the Weatherbox and gave me one of his sneeriest sneers. John-Joe pointed his shotgun at Mum. Neetch's back arched so high I thought his spine would snap. Mrs. Fitzgerald stood in front of Tony, sitting on the wall, one hand still covering his ear, looking up at her in holy terror.

"Now," she said. "This has taken long enough." She pointed at the Weatherbox. "Make it ring," she told him.

"You're not welcome here," Mum said, and went and

stood right in front of her. I think that was the bravest thing I've ever seen anyone do.

"Scarce are the places that welcome me," said Mrs. Fitzgerald. "Why would I expect any different here? I go where I go, and need no welcomes."

"I suppose that means you've none for us, then, either, Holly, dear?" said Hazel from the wall. Mrs. Fitzgerald's head snapped up, her eyes widened in shock.

"Aren't you going to introduce us to our brother-in-law?" asked Ash.

"And our nephew? I'm sorry, but our invitations to the wedding must have been lost in the post!" added Hazel.

"And to the christening!" put in Ash.

"You!" said Mrs. Fitzgerald. Her eyes narrowed and her lips grew thin. Hugh and John-Joe looked at each other uneasily.

"Who are they, Mum?" asked Hugh.

I slipped the bow over my head and climbed down the side of the phone box.

"You do not belong here," Mrs. Fitzgerald said. "This is none of your concern. Who stirs the pool? Who sings to the beast?"

"The beast will keep," said Hazel.

"We're sick of songs, anyway," said Ash.

"And of stirring," finished Hazel.

"You're the one who doesn't belong!" I cried, running up

and standing beside Mum. "You're the one who isn't welcome! Go away!"

Mrs. Fitzgerald tore her eyes away from her sisters and looked down at me. "Don't you want the line fixed?" she said. "Don't you want the year to have an Autumn? Barely a day late and already the cycle of Seasons is close to breaking. What chaos would be unleashed on the world if they no longer held to the old agreement? Can you not feel their approach? The air is thick with their presence. They have left their allotted quarters and come to pass judgment on the Weatherman. The Weatherman who failed to bring in the Autumn, who unleashed his forbidden powers and deserted his Doorway."

"Even if you get the line working," Mum said, her voice tight. "Even then, the Autumn can't come through without the Weatherman."

"Oh, but the Autumn is coming." She gestured to the east. "It will be here soon."

"That's not the right way—"

"No. It isn't," Mrs. Fitzgerald interrupted. "They are angry now, and when they get here they will be beyond all human reason. I wouldn't want to be the Weatherman, or his kin. So, either the agreement fails and the Seasons wander at will across the face of the world, or a new Weatherman steps forward."

"That's Neil!" I said. "Neil is the next Weatherman. Not you!"

"You keep quiet!" Hugh shouted. "You'll learn how to keep quiet when you come to live with us!"

Mum's eyes went wide and her lips went thin with rage. I saw her hands clench into fists. "No," she said. "You can't have her."

"Oh, yes." Her voice so calm and cool and reasonable, but with every word you could feel fear in the small of your back and the nape of your neck—cold and sharp. I could feel my teeth grinding together, not because I was angry or frustrated, but because I was scared. But she wasn't looking at me or Mum. She was looking at her sisters. "I am claiming Liz as my own. She's worth more than the rest of you put together, and I always wanted a sister for Hugh— just as I had sisters. She'll learn more and do more and see more with me than she ever could on her own, or with you. WHY ARE YOU NOT FIXING THE LINE?" It wasn't a shout. It was like her voice was a whip made of ice. Clive jumped like a startled frog, and lurched back to the hole. Bob and Cherie hurried to help. Tony tried to stand up, but John-Joe pushed him down flat on his back. The clouds were moving in from the horizon. Everything was getting darker and stranger.

Neetch was going wild, shaking and shivering, hissing

and screeching and spitting, his size shooting up and down. Owen tried to calm him, stroking his fur and whispering gently.

Mrs. Fitzgerald's face contorted and she lashed out with her left hand. Out of her palm came a stream of brambles and thorns that flew straight at Owen and Neetch. I grabbed for her arm but something threw me back with great force. I jumped to my feet and drew my bow. Mum pulled me back. But it was all right—the brambles and thorns tangled in a huge knot against a wall of woven willow trunks that suddenly sprang from the ground in front of Owen and Neetch. Hazel and Ash, standing now on top of the phone box, lowered their hands.

"Leave him alone!" said Owen, scrambling out from behind all the sudden vegetation. "He's my friend!"

"Creatures like that have no friends, boy," Mrs. Fitzgerald snarled. "Their hearts are black. Their minds are twisted and hungry and cunning. Why did you bring it here?"

"Oh, Holly, dear," said Hazel. "He's our friend, too."

"Our cat! Our foolish, stupid cat!" said Ash. "Oh, Holly, dear, we missed you so! Awfully! Terribly!"

The hags stared down from the top of the phone box. They were as young and as fresh as mountain streams, now—as young as Neil and me. Their faces white as drifts of snow, their eyes dark, their smiles wicked. Hazel sat with her legs crossed at the ankle, bare feet kicking out and back. Ash stood with her hands behind her back and her head cocked to one side.

"What are you doing here?" said Mrs. Fitzgerald. "I've done so much and worked so hard for this. Why work against me?"

"Why, we're here to send you home, dear!" said Hazel.

"The Black Pool needs you, dear!" said Ash.

"Send?" repeated Mrs. Fitzgerald. "You want to send me back?"

"Yes!" said Hazel. "We like it out here. Fresh air and green grass and nice people and being young again! You've had years of it. Years! While we sang and stirred in the cold dark. It's your turn!"

"You didn't even ask! Left without asking, you did! We'd have let you go. We could have taken turns. But, no. You deserted us! *Ochón, ochón,* we wept and wailed liked *oinseachs* for a year and a day. Now it's our turn for freedom! You're going home, and we're staying to enjoy hot showers and cooked breakfasts."

"No," said Mrs. Fitzgerald. "You don't understand. You don't see. When I'm Weatherman, I'll not stir and I'll not sing in a stone shell to a black hole. And neither will you. I was going to come for you. I was going to take you out of there."

"Were you?" said Hazel. "Oh, sister dear, how kind and thoughtful!"

"But, my dear," said Ash. "With us frolicking free in the world and you ruling the weather, even the blind and senile old beast is sure to notice sooner or later that he's all alone with a CD player and a charmed stick. What then?"

"It won't be alone," said Mrs. Fitzgerald, and she looked quickly down at me, and away. My breath caught in my throat and a cold black pit opened in my stomach.

"Never," said Mum.

"The Autumn has not come and the Summer is gone," Mrs. Fitzgerald said. "This *is* never."

"Got it!" said Clive from the hole. "All done! Er, just have to ring now and, er . . ."

"Ring!" commanded Mrs. Fitzgerald.

Clive pulled out a mobile phone and dialed. Everyone waited in silence. If Mum hadn't been holding me up I would have fallen over. "Yeah, uh, listen," Clive said. "I need you to reactivate a line for me here. Let me just give you the location and the authorization." He reeled off a string of numbers.

"It'll be soon," Mrs. Fitzgerald said. "I'll be Weatherman, and I'll take her and I'll teach her and she can take your place. Just wait. Go back. What difference will one more year make? When you come back out, the whole world will be ours."

"No you won't!" I yelled. "No it won't! No I won't!"

"My dear," said Hazel sadly. "That does sound nice. How wonderful that would be! So thoughtful! But we don't want to be ruled by you anymore."

"And we like Liz," said Ash. "We like them all. They gave us showers and breakfasts and eight channels of television. All you've ever given us was a thousand years of the cold and the dark with mad heads on us from listening to the whispers of that awful old beast."

"Then what do you think you are going to do?" asked Mrs. Fitzgerald. "My powers have grown with the years. Even the two of you together with that wretch of yours could not match me now."

"No," said Hazel. "We couldn't. We won't. But we will fight you."

"Oh, yes. Fight, fight, fight!" agreed Ash.

Mrs. Fitzgerald drew herself up. Her eyes flashed. "Try me, then."

Hazel laughed. "Not yet, you silly!"

"We're waiting for them, of course," said Ash.

"Them?" asked Mrs. Fitzgerald, glancing at the sky. "When they get here they'll make me Weatherman. If you can't make me go back now, what chance can you possibly have then?"

"Oh, not *them*, dear," said Hazel.

"Our friend Ed!" explained Ash.

"And his truck!" added Hazel.

"Oh, you're not Weatherman yet, dear!" said Ash.

"Done!" said Clive.

There was a silence. The clouds filled the sky. Night had fallen. Purple, green, and red light washed over everyone's faces.

John-Joe lifted the shotgun and aimed it at us. Hugh made fists of his hands and held them up. Behind them, shapes began to appear in the air above the road—elementals that Hugh was shaping into monsters. Claws of ice. Bodies of wind. Heads of fog. Mum and I stepped backward, my shoulder rubbing her elbow. Owen was behind me, and Neetch slunk around like a snake on legs. We heard a far-off rumble, then the sudden, shrill sound of the phone ringing. Mum gasped and we both jumped. Mrs. Fitzgerald took a step toward the Weatherbox with her hand raised, reaching for the small brass handle that opened the door. I aimed my arrow right at her, and Mum sketched shapes in the air with her fingers.

Mrs. Fitzgerald laughed. "They're nearly here," she said.

"Oh, they're here," said Hazel, and the hag girls leaped like salmon, and something roared and a blinding white light filled the air and the shattering sound of a horn blasted like the end of the world.

Mrs. Fitzgerald whirled away, and we jumped the wall, Owen grabbing Neetch as he went.

There was an awful tearing, crashing noise as the truck ploughed through the Weatherbox. The sides of the box spread out like a pair of wings. Glass and wood and plastic flew. The wings seemed to clutch the front of the truck as it swung around and slid sideways along the road, smoke coming from its wheels. The Weatherbox, flattened, was wrapped around the front of the truck. The telephone, crushed to pieces, lay on the road behind it, wires running back to the ragged square where the Weatherbox had stood, and down into the ground.

The ringing had stopped.

PART 4

The Maloneys and the Lake of Rain

CHAPTER 23

NEIL

The Weatherbox got bigger and closer. The beams from the headlights seemed to pull it toward us, or us toward it. All the little glass squares flashed twenty pairs of lights right back at us. I was expecting time to slow down. I wanted time to slow down. It didn't.

The Weatherbox crumpled, torn inside out, squashed flat against the windscreen. A second after that happened I heard the noise, the terrible, final crunch, and felt the all-destroying bump. Ed spun the wheel and jammed his foot down on the brakes, and I was thrown against Dad who was bracing himself against the door.

The truck hissed and jerked to a stop. I stared in shock at the mess, at the inside of the phone box. Our phone box, our Weatherbox, our magic, spread across the windscreen of Ed's truck like a bird made of glass and wood, broken and shattered. Oh my God. What had we done?

"Now," Dad said opening the door and sliding out. "Go, Neil, go!"

There was a scream of wind like a passing train and the door was ripped away with a screeching tear of metal. Dad was whipped away with it, out and up like a rag doll. The phone box was torn away from the front of the truck and sent cartwheeling down the road like a crash-landing kite.

A thick coat of ice crept down the windscreen. Ed was getting himself out on his side, and I slid across the seat to the hole where the passenger door had been. In front of the truck, three Shieldsmen in glowing, flying animal shapes were busy attacking an elemental. They were screaming and howling and laughing, leaping, and jumping and slashing and cutting while the elemental tried to fend them off with more gusts of fog. I grabbed hold of the wing mirror and leaned out, waiting for a gap in the battle.

Above the woods and the hill, all the clouds swept together and swirled, angry and blazing with light. They piled in closer and closer, a great rim of yellow sky all around them.

I heard a thump, and the young hag girl in the white dress landed on the windscreen.

"Hello," I said.

"Hello," she said, sideways, on all fours, her hands and her bare feet on the icy glass, her head tilted, her hair falling down over the grill, smiling.

"I'm Hazel," she said.

"I'm Neil," I said.

"Are you here to join the fight?" she said.

"Sort of," I said. "There's a plan. I'm going to the lake."

"OK," she said, and looked up over her shoulder. "Just one thing." Then she was gone.

Two white shapes shot above the crest of the hill—the girl hags in their dresses, arms outstretched, grabbing on to someone dark, outlined against the red and the purple and the green.

Mrs. Fitzgerald must have been shocked when we destroyed the Weatherbox. If she had flown the very second the truck hit, she would have reached the lake first and won. But she hadn't, and her sisters flew fast, too. Now they held her by her feet, slowing her, stopping her.

A greenish-gold glow brightened the dark and Dad, trailing vines and leaves and willow branches, flew up from wherever the wind had carried him. Birds and insects swirled around him. He passed the three sisters and turned at the crest of the hill. Mrs. Fitzgerald kicked, and the girl hags tumbled away from her, falling fast, down into the trees, their bodies limp, their hair streaming.

Before they struck they swerved, and swirling gusts of Summer wind sent by Dad carried them safely across the road and lowered them gently onto our lawn.

Dad and Mrs. Fitzgerald faced each other. He was covered in a golden glow, she shimmered with a cold blue light. The glow and the light grew stronger and met. There was a blinding flash, and the real war started.

I dropped down to the road. The battle between the Shieldsmen and the elementals was a confusion of fog and wind and rain and flying rainbow figures, all rushing furiously about between me and the woods. A gust of wind nearly knocked me off my feet, and ribbons of lightning danced wildly on the road.

"Look what you did," Liz growled beside me, fitting an arrow and firing it at a frozen elemental that was lobbing hailstones everywhere. The arrow chipped a chunk of ice off its head and the Shieldsmen gave a cheer.

"It was Dad's idea! I'm supposed to—aaagh!"

We dived apart as a burst of lightning shot out of the fog and struck the truck in a shower of sparks, leaving a black scorch mark on the metal.

"Oh, Ed won't like that," I said.

"The Shieldsmen are cool," Liz said.

"They're not bad."

The elementals retreated, pushed back into the woods by the fury of the Shieldsmen, leaving pools of melting ice and snow and burning patches of tar and scorched and broken trees. The van was on fire and big chunks had been knocked out of our wall. Over the woods Dad and Mrs. Fitzgerald were turning, turning, a long wide stretch of greenery against a long wide stretch of darkness.

Beyond the hill, the towering cloud columns lit up everything with their garish colors.

"OK," I said, my heart sinking. "I have to go."

"Lead the way," Liz said.

"Hold up," Mum said. "Where do you two think you're going?"

I told her Dad's plan as quickly as I could, horribly aware of every moment that passed. I somehow managed to do it without tying my tongue in knots.

"Come on!" Liz said." We've got to get going!"

"Nobody's going anywhere!" Mum roared.

"But, Mum!" I wailed.

"Except you," she said, pointing at me.

"And all of you," she said, pointing at the Shieldsmen.

"But, Mum!" Liz wailed.

"Stay. Where. You. Are," Mum told her. "And you Shieldsmen, guard him with your lives."

"WE WILL!" they all roared, snapping to attention.

"I'll come, too," said Hazel.

"But she broke our powers," said the other.

"So I'm not much use," said Hazel.

"But we don't want to be left behind," said the other.

Mum looked down at me. I tried to think of something to say. My mind had been roaring, one long loud roar since, oh God, since they arrested me at the forest and I thought they were going to lock me up forever. But that had just been shock and fear, the pit of my stomach full of rocks. Then Dad in the station. Dad, Dad, Dad attacking a police station for me, me, me and now Dad couldn't be Weatherman anymore because of me, me, me, but first he had to fight her, her, her and he might die, die, die! I couldn't take this. I couldn't take this.

Mum couldn't say anything, either. She gathered me up in a big tight hug, then let me go and nodded at the woods.

"Go on then. See you on the other side."

"Yeah," I said, and was carried away from her by a stampeding herd of Shieldsmen. I ran, dodging the flying legs and the masks and the stilts. Through the flapping kilts and thundering feet, a pale white shape slipped and dodged until she was beside me. Hazel grinned the sort of grin you grin when you've lost something you needed or loved and now you might as well make the best of carrying on without it. I grinned back, the sort of grin you grin when you're glad to have someone your own size along with you because you're surrounded by whooping muscled lunatics. We crashed along the forest path.

CHAPTER 24

LIZ

They ran into the woods and left us behind with the road full of smoking holes and covered in wrecked equipment, burning cars, a crashed truck, and a smashed Weatherbox.

It was very, very quiet.

"Mum," I said.

Ed's truck gave a cough, and the engine turned, caught, and throbbed loudly.

"There we go!" Ed called, leaning out of the cab. "It'll take more than a few scratches to put her off the road! Who wants a lift?"

"I'll pay you," Tony Holland said. "I'll pay you a thousand euros to get me out of here. Please."

"Er, what about us?" asked Clive.

"Them, too, if they'll fit," Tony said, gesturing to the other AtmoLabbers.

"You're not going anywhere!" said Mum. "If Ed's taking anyone it's Liz and Owen and Ash! They're children!"

"Oh, now you're worried about the children, are you, after sending your own son off into the woods with those head cases? Get into the truck, you lot."

Ed jumped down in front of Tony.

"Nobody," he said, "gets in my truck without my permission."

"A thousand euros!" shouted Tony. "Two thousand!"

"Have you no shame?" yelled Mum.

I turned my back on the argument, feeling tired and sore and let down and left out. I gripped my bow and looked into the woods. I could dash in while no one was looking. I could catch up. I could be one of the Shieldsmen, fighting Hugh's monsters. Before the thought had finished crossing my mind I was leaning forward, ready to run, when I realized that someone had somehow got in front of me. Ash was staring into the woods, small and lost and alone, no bigger than Owen and delicate as a glass doll. Neetch padded up and rubbed against her ankle. Owen came up and leaned against me. I put my arm around his shoulder. It was dark now, despite the lights from the clouds.

"Cat," Ash said, her voice fond and gentle and delicate. "Bad cat."

She turned and blinked up at me. There was a cut on her forehead, a bruise on her cheek, and her dress was torn and muddy.

"Hello," she said.

"Hi," I said.

"Where are you going?" she asked.

"I don't know," I said, and it was true. I couldn't really go into the woods. That was Neil's fight.

The argument around the truck had died down. I heard them approaching, Ed's heavy steps hurrying cross the road.

"Ash? Is that you? Ash, are you OK? What happened? Where's Hazel?" he asked her.

"Silly Ed," she said with a giggle. Then her face fell. "My bad sister hurt us, Ed. She did something to us. I can't remember. I'm trying, but it's hard. She broke us. She wants to take us back to the mountains and chain us down and make us sing and stir. Then, with the Weathergirl here, there'd be three of us again. I don't want to sing and stir a mean old black hole forever! Stop her, Ed! Stop her, cat! Stop her, Weathergirl!"

I stopped breathing. "What did you call me?"

"It's OK," Ed said. "The Weatherman and Neil will stop her. Come with me, honey. You'll be warm in the truck."

"Yeah," Cherie said. "We gotta get you off this road."

"They'll lose," Ash said, sad and solemn. "Neil will never

be Weatherman. She will, and then she'll do what she wants—to us and to you. They won't let Neil be Weatherman because they're too mad at the Weatherman. They don't care what she's like or what she's done to anybody else."

"How do you know all this?" I asked.

She looked at me, utterly miserable. "I know lots of things. Lots and lots. But she's made me start to forget them all. They're all going away. I can't remember how to talk to flowers. I can't remember how to draw a song. I can't remember the shapes of the seven rocks. I can't remember my own name, my secret name. It's so hard, but I'm trying to remember just this: they will depose the Weatherman. They will reject his appointed heir out of rage at your father. They will accept my bad sister . . ." She grabbed my arm and whispered urgently, "Unless there's someone else, Weathergirl."

"But why would they take m—why would they take anyone else, over her?" I demanded.

"Because they don't know what she's done to *them*!" she hissed. "My bad sister did something much worse than anything your father has done! Something that could make them forget how angry they are with him. But they don't know! She hid it! You hid it for her!"

I'd hidden her crime. All they knew was that the Seasons had failed to change, and that Dad had become

256

Summer. He could tell them it was all Mrs. Fitzgerald's fault, but would they believe him? Would they listen? Would they care? There had to be proof of what she had done. There had to be someone to explain. There had to be a witness.

And there was. But I'd buried it in a bog for her.

"The Baby Season!" I exclaimed. "We've got to save the Baby Season."

Ash put her tiny hand in mine. I looked back at Ed and Mum and AtmoLab. "Ed," I said. "Bring the truck. Follow us."

I started down the road, Ash holding one hand, Owen the other, and Neetch stalking ahead, tail waving. The air was thick, and a fog was creeping out of the trees.

We reached the Ditches at the same time as Ed pulled up in his truck. Mum was beside me, the AtmoLabbers trailing behind her and Tony Holland trailing behind them, complaining about his ear. Ed climbed down out of the truck, and we all stood on the verge of the road. The mist floated over the pools of water, lit up with the red and the green and the purple light from the Seasons. Reeds and ferns and tall grasses stood thin and sharp, and the willows drooped over secrets and shadows.

"Ed," I said, "do you have a rope?

"Yeah, in the truck. I'll go get it."

AtmoLab hung back a little, trying to listen in without

getting in the way. Tony went over and sat down against the wheel of Ed's truck.

"What do you need a rope for?" Mum asked.

"We're going fishing for a Season," I told her.

"Honey, is this the time? I know you want to get the poor thing out of there, but we really should be getting as far from here as we can until we hear from your dad that it's safe to come back."

"This is the time," said Ash. "It's a newborn Season. It's their child. If you save it, if you take it to them, they'll know what my bad sister did and she'll never be Weatherman. They'd scour this whole island to bare rock first. But the person who freed it, the Weathergirl who rescued it—oh, she, yes, *she* would be blessed above all others."

Ed came back with a thick coil of blue rope. "This do?"

"Yeah. Good. Thanks. I think we could tie one end around the Baby Season and one end around the truck, and pull it out, couldn't we?"

Ed, Bob, Cherie, and Clive all looked at each other and then back at me.

"I've got a better idea," Ed said.

"OK," I replied with a shrug. "But we have to get on with it!"

Ed had a block and tackle in the truck. A block and tackle is, like, a big thick rope with a sort of metal hook on it, and there's this other metal bit with another rope, and it all looks like something you'd use to go fishing for the Loch Ness Monster. So I thought, fine, we'll drop the hook in the water with a bit of bait attached and the Baby Season will bite and we'll drag it up. "What bait do you use for Baby Seasons? Would a worm do?" I asked Ed. Ed said he didn't know, but the little hag girl did.

"Weathergirls," she said. I pretended I hadn't heard her.

Everybody rushed and ran and worked together, quick and fast, and in only a few minutes Mum and Ed and Clive and Bob and Cherie were tying the bit they called the pulley to the trunk of a tree near the pool where the Baby Season had sunk. Or at least the one where I thought it had sunk. It was hard to be sure. I jumped around the grassy banks, splashing in the water and sinking down into the mud, while Owen and Ash and Neetch chased each other around and threw stones and sticks at the water, and Ash showed Owen how to weave little boats out of reeds and rushes.

Above us all were Summer Dad and Mrs. Fitzgerald, locked in battle, and the Seasons—huge flying towers of clouds and colors, each as wide as a city.

Ed pulled the rope through the pulley and tied it to the trunk of the tree.

The bog was eerie and strange and dark, shining with light but full of shadows, and all the pools that we used to think were just muddy ditches seemed deep and silent and sinister, with ribbons of fog floating over them. I jumped up and down and stamped my feet to work out my impatience. It all took only ten minutes, fifteen at the most, but it felt like hours were crawling by and the world was ending without us.

I tried to reach out to the Baby Season under the water. "Hold your breath. Close your eyes. Close your mouth. Don't be afraid. We're coming down. We'll get you out. We'll set you free, little baby thing, little baby thing way down in the dark."

Tony Holland limped down from the road, moaning at everyone. He was holding a handkerchief to his ear. There wasn't even that much blood on it. "I could get an infection!" he whined. "I need a doctor. I need painkillers. Stop what you're doing! Stop! I'll fire the lot of you! Why are you helping these people? They shot me with an arrow!"

"They only did what we've wanted to do every day for the last two years, Tony," Bob said.

Up the hill a bit, lightning suddenly flashed and winds blew, and branches snapped like matchsticks, as if there were some big mad bear charging through the woods chased by a thundercloud. Lights blazed and glowed and darted like they were alive, and gushes of wind and water exploded through the treetops.

"Hurry!" I said.

"Here we go," Cherie said, putting a foot against the

tree and pulling the last knot tight. Ed held the rope with the hook at the end, looking down into the pool.

"Now," he said, "we'll just drop this down and hope it grabs hold, and then we pull it out, right?"

"Right," I said.

"Needs bait," said the little girl hag, and I sighed.

"Yeah," I said, and I took the hook and the rope out of Ed's hands, sucked in a deep breath, and jumped, feet first, down into the cold black waters of the bog.

CHAPTER 25

NEIL

The light under the trees was insane. All the raging colors of the Seasons flashed and flowed as they whirled around in a great, slow swirl, angry and impatient. A mist was rising, coming out of the ground and thickening between the trees. We had started to spread out a bit along the path.

"Stay together!" Weisz yelled.

Hazel ran beside me. I hoped her feet would be OK. I wouldn't have liked to run through misty woods in my bare feet. I wished I'd nipped into the house and got her a pair of Liz's old runners. She stumbled.

"Help me," she said, and I reached out and we joined hands and ran together. There was some part of me that was saying, look, the world is ending and you are going to die, and a pale and night-haired girl with eyes as dark and deep as a shaded pool is holding your hand of her own free will and showing no sign of letting go. For God's sake, keep hold of that girl until the very crack of doom, because the end of the world and dying suck, but holding her hand doesn't.

We were moving fast and covering ground. Already, through the whiteness, I could see the main path that cut across the length of the wood up ahead.

"There!" I shouted. "We're nearly halfway to the wall!"

We leaped from the trees and over a small drainage ditch, onto the path. I slowed, searching the other side for the trail that would take us up the hill. Hazel's hand was still in mine, and she pulled me to a stop. The Shieldsmen spread across the path, their hands slightly out from their sides, their masks covering their faces, their bodies crouched. Things were moving in the fog. Hugh's elementals came down onto the path.

There was an explosion, a brilliant blue blaze of wild lightning. Crackling arcs of sizzling electricity reached for us. One of the Shieldsmen was blown back into the trees when an arc struck his chest.

And I thought, *Is this how it's going to be? Are they going to fight and maybe even die for me while I just duck and run? I'm supposed to be the Weatherman, now!*

Weather, weather, weather rushed in at us from all sides. Bone-crunching blasts of air. Waves of rain that turned to ice and fell like knives. Forked arcs of blazing electricity. *Brilliant!* I thought. *Knives and forks!*

The Shieldsmen were fast and bright and beautiful. They flung themselves at the elementals, flying and changing, growing into their long, sleek animal shapes, their claws and teeth shining through the fog and the ice.

I shut my eyes. I reached out with my mind. I left my body crouched behind a rock and saw the Shieldsmen and the elementals grapple and fight and slash. The Shieldsmen could duck and dive and dodge most of the things the elementals threw at them, and if they hit them right they could break them apart. But the elementals flew back together as fast as they were broken, and they were getting better and their aim was improving. They conjured a waterspout out of the air and froze it, and a thousand slivers of ice like nails lashed the Shieldsmen, leaving them cut and bleeding.

I tried, but I couldn't stop the elementals. They were closed off from me, slaves to Hugh through his mother and the Baby Season. I needed elementals of my own, but the idea of enslaving them to do my bidding was revolting. And, anyway, I already had a loyal, free, magical army. I just needed to trust, keep my head down, and give them a helping hand.

Weisz, the eagle, rallying after the ice nails, opened his beak, and a streak of lightning shot out and blew an elemental away. A Shieldsmen-wolf howled like the north wind and a gale sent an elemental spinning into the sky. The fly buzzed and a torrent of rain flattened another into a muddy pool. The seagull snapped her wings and a roll of thunder like a cannonball shattered a wall of ice. The Shieldsmen closed in on the remaining elementals, and Hazel pulled my hand.

I fell back into my head, dizzy and a bit sick. She dragged me across the path and into the trees, up toward the crown of the hill.

Trees around us were creaking and bending and shaking. Billows of thick fog blew past us and around us. Hailstones as big as my fist hammered down on our backs and our legs and heads, leaving bruises, drawing blood.

"It's such a pity you can't fly," the girl hag said. We were breathing hard and aching from head to foot.

"You can fly, can't you?" I said between gasps. "Maybe you could give me a lift?"

"Not anymore," she said. "I can't do anything anymore. Sorry."

"Don't be," I said. "When all this is over, I'm going to get you a pair of shoes. Flying's all well and good, but when it comes to walking you can't beat a pair of shoes."

We left the fight behind. The world got quieter and less violent and things stopped falling out of the sky and hurting us, though we could still hear the sizzling and crackling and roaring down below. We reached the wall and climbed over it, and I saw that Hazel's bare feet were cut and bruised and muddy.

I turned my back toward her. "Get up," I said.

"What?"

"Get up. Haven't you ever played piggyback?"

"Not in . . . a long time."

"Come on, then. Before Hugh finds us."

She climbed up on my back, and I carried her down through the strip of woodland above the farm. There was no sign of Hugh until we came to the edge of the trees. He was standing just beyond, in grass up to his waist, between us and the lake. Over the lake were the huge continents of clouds and light that were the angry Seasons.

The man on the radio had talked about downbursts and lightning and tornadoes, but apart from the occasional flicker, the undersides of the cloud columns did nothing but glower and boil, spreading around the edges into flat, sinister hazes. The Seasons were holding back, for now, but, if someone didn't sort out the Doorway soon, they might really lose their tempers and then we'd have that super-mega-terror-storm the other radio guy had been so excited about. Dad and Mrs. Fitzgerald were still up there, somewhere, lost in the vastness.

"Put her down," Hugh said. "Your hippies have wrecked all my elementals, so I'm going to have to boil you alive myself."

"Do you want to get down?" I asked Hazel.

"No," she said. "I'm happy where I am."

"OK," I said. I stared at Hugh, and he stared back at me. Tiny elementals shimmered around us like a beaded curtain. The strip of grass that stretched from him to us was turning yellow. Hugh was heating the air between us, his elementals stoking it like a furnace. A flare of dry heat that wilted every living thing it touched struck us, and we curled like Autumn leaves, surrounded by a storm of wavering, dancing air. It was like being trapped in the middle of a desert mirage. When we breathed in, it was like swallowing red-hot balls of cotton wool wrapped in barbed wire. The grass was crisping, blackening, smoking.

My mind reaching out beyond the wall of heat, pulling elementals to me.

Cold, I told them. *Cold, cold, cold.*

My skin prickled as a layer of cool air settled around us, but the heat kept rising, and I felt it burning through the cool. Blinking in the shimmering haze, I could see that Hugh's shirt was soaked in sweat. He hadn't been very precise with his heat wave. He had caught himself in the wall of hot air meant for us. He was swaying on his feet, trying to dismiss the heat, but it was like a chain reaction, rising beyond his control, rising and roasting. He collapsed.

I put my head down and charged like a bull down the strip of smoking grass. The tip of a single blade glowed as an ember flared, and everything ignited at once. Flames exploded around us, eating everything they touched, sucking all the oxygen from the air, chasing us down the long strip of grass as we stomped toward Hugh. Even with our layer of cold turned to deep freeze I could feel the scorching heat of the firestorm as it bore down on us and I bore down on Hugh.

A fierce, sudden wind lifted the flames higher, roaring and whirling around and around, faster and faster, walls of speeding flame, twisting and turning.

My legs gave out, and I fell to my knees and slid down the last of the slope to where Hugh had curled up into a ball, hands clasped around his head, calling for his mum. I pushed the layer of cold elementals out to cover him, too.

Cold, cold, cold, I told them.

Hazel's arms were wrapped tight around my neck, her face buried in my shoulder. We were gasping in air that seared our throats and lungs, utterly exhausted, half roasted—the three of us now at the bottom of a burning tornado. If my elementals got any colder we'd all die of frostbite.

I knew, in that moment, that we had seconds to live.

CHAPTER 26

LIZ

There's an amazing difference between being dry, or just a little bit damp, and being completely wet and getting wetter by the second. It's one thing when you're jumping into a swimming pool or taking a shower, and you're ready for it and all you have to do is get out, or turn it off and find a warm towel. It's another thing when you're fully dressed and you're in it from head to toe and getting deeper and deeper and you're not at all sure about getting out.

It was pitch black and it was filthy and it was freezing, and, in the first few seconds, or even minutes, I wasn't thinking about finding the Gray Thing or holding my breath or anything, I was just looking at the only things I could see, which were loads and loads of bubbles running fast in front of my face. I remembered something Mum had once told me about how, if I was underwater and I got turned until I wasn't sure which way was up and which was down, all I had to do was blow some bubbles from my mouth and the direction they went in would always be up. So I could tell which way was up, and I knew I had to go in the opposite direction.

I kicked my legs and moved my arms and turned and twisted until I was swimming down. I could feel the rope in my hand, or I thought I could, through the cold and the mud. All I had to do now was keep going down until I found the Baby Season. How hard could that be? It was a bog hole. Bog holes weren't that deep. Or were they?

I swam. Down and down. Or was it? I couldn't tell if I was moving at all. Maybe I was just floating in place. Maybe my legs were still sticking out of the surface of the bog hole and everyone was staring at them as they kicked and kicked and me with my head stuck in the mud. Any second now they would grab hold of me and pull me out.

No. I was going down, and the mud was getting thicker all around me. There were no bubbles now. I groped ahead, feeling for the Baby Season. Poor Baby Season, down here in the dark and the mud. At least it didn't have to breathe.

Thicker and thicker. Slimy and cold and sticky. I was clawing, digging, pulling myself down like a worm, burrowing deeper. I wriggled and pushed, blind, freezing, breath all gone, mud squeezing me tight—too tight to move. I was going to drown. I was going to die. I was going to open my mouth and try to breathe and all the mud would rush in and fill my lungs. I'd be stuck down here until they dug me up.

I pushed with everything I had. My hand was stretched out in front of me, and I felt something solid. I pushed again, my whole body shuddering, and it crumbled and broke and I fell through—into light and air.

Under me was a carpet of clouds. White mountains and gray valleys and deep pits that fell away to a far-off green-ness. All around me was blue, bright and fierce and clear, and roaring with breath like endless laughter. Above me was dark where the air and the light ended.

I think I had fallen into the Baby Season's mind—into its memories.

———•—

And there, shining in the dark, was the burning life star that roars energy and light into the world—the shining mouth that sings everything into being. And I was part of the song, and the song was movement, always movement, forever rising and forever falling. A sky dance, the great-est of all dances, and as I danced the sky dance I forgot everything except the incredible joy of sky dancing. I rose with the warm air; fell with the cool. I turned in the wind

271

and flew through a terrible, raging storm. I let it rage, then let it die. Clouds dissolved until there was clear still air, and I soared through the clear still air. There was no yesterday and no tomorrow, just this, until the cool air stirred and clouds appeared and began their long steady march, drifting a veil of rain beneath. And this was all there ever was or would be, just this fierce unending happiness until . . .

. . . something took hold of my hand—took hold of it, or was I already holding it? I knew I could let it go and just be there forever, dancing joyfully in the light and dark, hot and cold, air and electricity, with the shining mouth singing to me and singing to everything. I wanted to dance forever. I wanted to let the hand go, but another hand closed around my arm and pulled me up into the dark where I felt I wasn't supposed to go—up where there was no air and only dead cold and the song couldn't be heard.

My mouth filled with mud.

I couldn't even choke or cough. I definitely couldn't breathe. My arm was being pulled from its socket and there was weight all around me. I knew I couldn't hold on to the hook and the rope for much longer. I just couldn't.

Gradually, the mud got thinner, turned into black water,

and now I could cough it out of my throat and mouth, but I still couldn't breathe. I went limp as water filled me up. I wondered if they would send me back down. I wondered if they would be angry because I hadn't saved the Baby Season.

Then I was on my hands and knees in the middle of the bog hole, coughing water out of my mouth and trying to gasp in air. My throat was raw and my chest was on fire and there were hands holding me up and clapping me on the back. But the bog hole I had just swum to the bottom of now only came up to my elbows, even though I was sinking a little into the muck underneath.

It wasn't deep at all.

And I hadn't got the Baby Season.

Mum and Ed helped me crawl to the edge of the hole and sit with my head between my knees, more water streaming out of me and off me.

There must have been a branch or a tree down there that had caught around me somehow, or maybe it was the rope all tangled about me, but it was tight and heavy on my shoulders and my back. I tried to twist and shrug it off, but it wouldn't move.

"Help," I said, hoarse and tired and soaked, freezing with the cold and ready to start crying in a minute from how horrible everything was. "Please, help."

"Liz," Mum said. "You did it."

I blinked up at her. No, she was wrong. I hadn't done anything except . . . I remembered something to do with a song, a dance and flying forever and . . . For a moment I had been a Season. I had ruled the sky. Oh, my heart. My heart, it broke. I opened my mouth and moaned because I had lost it—the wild mad song and dance. "Oh, Mummy, Mummy, it's gone . . ." I wailed.

"Tell her to be quiet," John-Joe said.

I didn't care. I didn't care that he was standing there on the other side of the bog hole with his shotgun and the AtmoLabbers kneeling in a row with their hands on their heads, and Owen and Ash huddled together beside them with Neetch crouched between. The loss hurt too much. Mum knelt and wiped my face and hushed me, and Ed on my other side took the rope and the hook out of my numb, shivering hand. He had to open my fist finger by finger, and underneath was another fist, and that's when I realized that there had been another hand closed around mine—a thin gray hand, and an arm lying along mine. I turned my head, and lying on my shoulder was the narrow little head of the Gray Thing. It was sitting on me, riding piggyback, wrapped around me.

"You did it," Mum said again.

"Yeah," John-Joe said. "You did it. And now you can go and put the flippin' thing back."

CHAPTER 27

NEIL

The tiny bubble of cool air I was fighting to keep around us shrank and grew in time with my breathing. It was as if we'd been flung into one of those coal-fired boiler engines and were surviving by spitting on the coals to put them out. But they kept reigniting, and I was running out of spit. The air froze and melted, froze and melted, freezing a little less and melting a little more each time. It might have been easier if I hadn't made the bubble big enough to cover Hugh, too. Hazel had climbed down off my back and we crouched close together right over his moaning head, but even so, realistically, my bubble was going to die long before the fire did.

The first drops on my back were close to boiling, and they were big and thick and heavy enough to leave bruises. Then the rain came thicker and faster and colder and the smoke swept around with the flames, and then the flames were gone and the wind died and the rain hammered on as we coughed and hacked and wheezed and tears streamed down our faces.

The smoke parted around us and before us, bending up and away as two figures emerged from the swirling darkness together—Dad and Mrs. Fitzgerald.

"We agreed to a truce," Dad said. "When we saw you were all in danger, we agreed to a truce. The truce will hold until we reach the lake together."

"Sorry, Dad," I said, feeling as though I had failed yet again.

"Not your fault, Neil. None of this is your fault."

"Mum?" Hugh said, finally looking up and realizing that he was alive. "Mum, look what he did! He wrecked all my elementals and then he burned our field and he nearly burned me!"

"The truce will hold," Mrs. Fitzgerald said. "The advantage is ours. The Weatherman will perform his final duty, then relinquish his position, and the Seasons will decide on his replacement: his wretched and tainted offspring, or a new family, powerful and reliable. The advantage is ours."

"We'll see," Dad replied.

They kept their eyes locked tight on each other.

"Come on, then," Dad said. "They're waiting."

"And angry," she said. "And getting angrier."

The fires had died, leaving steam and smoke everywhere, thicker than any fog. And the rain drove down into the glowing cinders and hot ashes. Back at the edge of the wood, the oak tree was now a blackened, smoking stump.

Dad pointed to a spot between himself and Mrs. Fitzgerald. The ground was covered with a thick layer of burnt grass that crumbled to hot ash under our feet. I refused to move until Hazel climbed onto my back again. She put her arms around my neck and rested her head on my shoulder. I could hear her breathing softly. Everything hurt. I could barely stand, I was so exhausted, but she felt like no weight at all. Hugh snorted, and we went and stood there and began to walk down toward the shore of the lake—Dad and Mrs. Fitzgerald moving slightly sideways, like a pair of lizards in a staring contest.

Over the lake the three Seasons in their cloud towers were slowly, ponderously turning. Way up high at the uppermost limits of the sky they all merged in a great flat cold mass that spread from horizon to horizon. The vivid colors that flashed and glowed in the clouds lit up the landscape below. Each of the three rotating columns was thick and wide at the top, growing thinner toward the bottom, until it tapered away to a tiny wisp that touched the surface of the lake and danced and moved like a flame in a breeze.

We reached the edge of the lake and stopped. I set Hazel down and she took my hand. Dad and Mrs. Fitzgerald held their stare for one long moment more, and then Dad turned and looked out at the lake and spread his arms wide and let the Summer go.

CHAPTER 28

LIZ

"Go on," John-Joe said. "Drop it back in. Go on!"

"Leave her alone!" Mum told him.

"I'll leave her alone when she does what I says!" He lifted the gun to his shoulder and pointed it at me. Mum and Ed both splashed into the bog hole in front of me.

"Get out of the way!" He swung the gun around, pointing it at Owen and Ash.

"OK," Ed said. "Look, we'll do what you say. We'll do it."

"Do it, then!"

Mum and Ed slowly and carefully took hold of the Baby Season. Ed got its arm and Mum got its body and they gently pulled.

"What's taking so long? Get it off and drop it back in, ye eejits!" John-Joe moaned.

"It won't come off!" Mum pulled and tugged, and Ed dragged at it and yanked, but it wouldn't budge. It wasn't even holding on that tight, and it didn't feel stuck or anything, the way a limpet sticks to a rock at the beach. It just would not move.

I shivered and shook. I felt the black bog muck drying my skin. I didn't care about any of it. I felt myself rock back and forth. "I fly big sky. I fly big sky. I fly big sky . . ." I chanted, trying to hold on to the memory of the sky dance under the bog hole.

"Hush, honey, hush," Mum said. "You have to help us."

John-Joe stalked around the bog hole to where I was sitting.

"If you don't get it off I'll throw them both in! I don't care! You hear, girlie? I said I'll drown you like a pup!"

"Get away from her!" shouted Mum.

John-Joe pointed the gun in her face and pushed her back, then he squatted down beside me like a fat old toad. His breath puffed like smoke and stank of something rotten and old and dead. "I'll put you both in, girlie, that's what I'll do. And do you know what I'll do then? Oh, it's a nice deep hole, it is. I'm thinking a deep hole like that could hold all of you. Every last one of you, and no one would ever find you down there with that precious thing. It's like bog butter. You know bog butter, don't you? They find lumps of it thousands of years old and it's still good for making a sandwich. That's what that thing is like—buried in the bog but still doing its job. Not the rest of you, though. You'll be more like them bog men, dried up old mummies, all black and withered. That's what I'm thinking. And I'll start with you, so I will. In you go, girlie!"

He grabbed my arm and lifted.

Just then, something yellow grew and spread behind the crown of the hill. A long thin ribbon of fire, dancing and bending, coming up from somewhere beyond the treetops and outlined against the glowing clouds. Even John-Joe paused to watch as the flame seemed to jump all across the top of the hill, a great black gush of smoke leaking out of it.

"Oh my God!" cried Mum. "Oh, Neil! Oh no!"

"Neetch!" I yelled. "Neetch help! Get him!"

John-Joe pushed. We splashed back into the bog hole, and I could feel the mud sink and deepen under me. John-Joe could too, because he dropped me and jumped for the edge as I sank down. The Baby Season on my back shifted, and I heard it whine softly in my ear.

"I'm sorry," I said. I wondered if we would fly again when we got down there, or if it had just been a dream—one of those dreams you have once in your whole life and then never again no matter how much you want it, or long for it, or try to remember what it was and what it felt like. Oh, well. I wouldn't be wanting or longing for much down in the black, anyway. The water closed around my head. I was so cold I couldn't feel it anymore.

Then something big splashed into the pool.

There were bubbles, and there was foam, and there was a shape, dripping with water and muck and dirt and weeds—a shape with huge yellow eyes and a mouth bursting with teeth like jagged knitting needles. And those needles, cruel and sharp and bigger than the bones in a tyrannosaur skeleton, closed around me as delicately and softly as a pair of oven gloves, and I was lifted out of the water and dropped gently on the edge of the bog hole, wiping the cold, dirty water from my face while Neetch, the bog-water frothing all around him, turned on John-Joe.

Neetch wasn't a cat. Neetch just kinda looked like a cat when he was small. Neetch was a bog beast—a bog beast as big as a house.

He was covered in long, thick shaggy fur like a woolly mammoth. His legs were tall and crooked and had six claws each. His tail was as long as his body and lashed the air behind him. His ears stretched back like a bat's, his whiskers drooped like a massive Victorian moustache, and his face was like a demon's. He climbed out of the bog hole, wrapped in a coat of mud, and hissed at John-Joe.

In his terror John-Joe must have jerked at the trigger of the shotgun. There were two sudden bursts of flame and smoke, two quick, stabbing cracks that hurt my ears and made everyone flinch and duck. Then John-Joe dropped the gun and ran into the trees. Neetch went after him, bounding into the fog, and then they were both gone, though we could hear them as they went crashing one after the other through the wood.

"Come on out of that," Ed said slowly, and he lifted me up and hugged me to his chest. We stood shivering and silent for a moment. Up on the hill, the ribbon of fire was gone and everything was covered in a thick gray layer of smoke and steam.

"I've got to get to the lake," I said. "I've got to get the Baby Season there."

"NO!" Mum said. "You're not going up there! Hugh and his elementals are up there in the woods, and John-Joe, and that fire . . . I'm not letting you go up there!"

"But, Mum . . ."

"She has to go," Ash said quietly.

"I can't let her!"

"Mum," I said. "I'm not—"

"You're not?" she said. "Good!"

"Then she will win," said Ash, sadly.

"No, she won't. Mum, I'm not going through the woods because that would be stupid. I'm going to ask Ed to drive me around in his truck. Ed, would you drive me around in your truck?"

"Sure," he said, but his voice was strained.

"Ed!" said Ash. "Ed?"

"It's OK," he said, bringing his hand, all covered in blood, around from his back. "Just a scratch. Oh, dear. Would you look at that?"

He wasn't talking about the blood. He was pointing at the hill.

One of the three cloud blocks was directly above us, and the other two were over to our left and to our right. All three had long, thin trailing wisps that ran down from their massive bases to vanish somewhere beyond the hill—at the lake, I guessed. Now a fourth thin cloud, like a jagged, crooked line drawn by a pencil, rose up into the southern sky, and started to spread, full of light.

"Summer," said Ash. "Summer is here. The Weatherman is at the lake."

CHAPTER 29

NEIL

A quivering wisp of light appeared on the lake, like a flame of burning gas. It turned, and danced, and rose. A cone of silvery dew full of a white light that broke into hazy, glittering rainbows quivering like flags, swirling up into the sky, churning and teeming, the rainbows spreading and merging into a titanic cone of glowing colors, taking its place with the other Seasons. Liz, Owen, and me had always loved rainbows. As children of the Weathermen they seemed like special signals from the Seasons meant just for us, bright, beautiful bridges we might one day climb to join them in the sky. This rainbow looked like the fang of a kaleidoscopic serpent biting into the water of the lake. The Summer was angry. The Summer was furious. The insult and indignity it had suffered would never be forgotten. Whatever happened next, I reckoned the chances of Ireland ever getting a decent Summer again were pretty slim.

Dad's light went out. I'd got so used to it I'd almost forgotten it was there. He shrank back down to ordinary Dad-size, small and dull and tired, barely able to stand on his own two legs.

Not that Mrs. Fitzgerald looked much better. The two of them had been fighting with powers that just didn't fit into human bodies or human minds. Her power, even boosted with what she'd stolen from her sisters, had been drained by the battle. Now her hair was snowy white, her face thin and lined, and her hands and fingers like crooked claws. I saw Hugh watching her, and a crafty, calculating look came into his eye: maybe it wouldn't be so long until he became Weatherman. I felt sick just looking at him.

Dad slowly waded out into the lake. By the time he reached the middle the water was up to his chest. He stopped, and looked up, and shut his eyes. The clouds boiled and gushed, the great cyclones turned, the colors flared too bright, and I covered my eyes. When I opened them again and blinked the light away, the colors were gone, and the clouds, and the cyclone. The change was so complete it was as if we had jumped to a different world. Now it was night, and a million stars had appeared, and the moon, full and bright, hung directly over the lake. Dad was standing perfectly still in the dead center of the moon's reflection. A single ripple floated away from him and through the four other figures that stood around him.

They were dim shadows in the moonlight, four or five times as big as Dad, standing in or hovering above the lake. One was sort of man-shaped, covered in lumps, all irregular, put together as if it were some sort of jigsaw. It was a body made up entirely of fruits and vegetables, all fitted together to make something that looked human, like a joke. I saw carrots and apples and oranges and bananas and leeks. Its fingers were zucchini. Its lips were pea-pods. Its eyes were some sort of flower. From its back grew two thick, crooked wooden limbs that split into smaller branches and twigs all covered with leaves, but the leaves were brown and withered and dead. Autumn.

To one side of Autumn was a huge, thick ring, braided out of shoots and creepers and ivy and weeds. It was constantly moving and shifting and changing as a hundred different creatures—mice, rats, birds, monkeys—crawled over it and clung to it and fluttered through it, weaving it into patterns and then unweaving it again, so it was growing and spreading and changing all the time. Its long green shoots trailed in the water, thick with pond weed and willow branches. It was like an elaborate mask, but never once in all its moving and changing did it even come close to looking human. Spring.

Winter was a constant steady fall of rain and snow and

287

perfectly round hailstones that never struck the lake but danced up and down the length of a shapeless column. Each raindrop was filled with silver moonlight, each snowflake glowed and fluttered, and each hailstone shone like a pearl. It looked like a living chandelier.

And Summer was a hot round ball of sparkling, glittering, flashing lightning, changing from bright blinding blue to blazing, angry red and back again. It seemed to lean toward Dad and reach for him with its lightning fingers, but Dad stood perfectly still in the middle, head up, shoulders back, looking proud. He wasn't sorry for what he'd done, so there was no point in trying to pretend he was.

They talked. I couldn't hear what was said. I mean, it wasn't really talking. They don't talk. It didn't take long. Dad bowed his head, and Summer sent a torrent of lightning scorching into the sky that lit up everything for miles around and blinded us and deafened us. Dad flinched and stumbled, going down under the water for a moment. Then Summer subsided and the others remained completely still, and Dad dragged himself out of the lake and fell onto the shore.

"Dad?" I said, squatting down beside him and putting a hand on his shoulder.

"It's done. I'm no longer Weatherman." He stopped, his voice choked, then he swallowed and went on, "Summer wanted to kill me. To boil me alive in the lake. The others decided I should live because of the long service of my family. But Neil, our family can no longer serve. I'm so sorry. They won't accept you. I don't think they ever will. It was all for nothing."

He sat in the mud with his feet in the water and his head in his hands. His wet hair plastered to his head seemed thin and gray now, his body gaunt and weak. I knelt beside him, my hand still on his shoulder.

"It doesn't matter," I said in a voice that didn't really seem to be mine at all. "As long as we're all OK. We're a tribe, Dad. We'll be together and we'll be OK."

I looked up at Hazel, but her hair fell about her face, and she sat down and drew her knees up and put her arms around her legs. Weisz and the Shieldsmen had emerged from the trees to join us. They looked grim. Would they have to serve Mrs. Fitzgerald now?

"Then it's mine," said Mrs. Fitzgerald, and she walked into the lake, where the four Seasons were waiting to make her their Weatherman.

CHAPTER 30

LIZ

Ed insisted on driving.

"It was only birdshot," he said, leaning on Mum. "No, really, it is just a scratch."

He wouldn't let anyone look at it or check it or put a bandage on it. I didn't argue because we didn't have time. Mum and I helped him, and we all hurried back through the bog to the road and pushed Ed up behind the wheel of the truck. Ash was very worried, but we couldn't listen to her because we could argue all night and then we wouldn't get to the lake or get Ed looked after either, so it seemed better just to hurry, whatever we did.

Owen stared into the woods after Neetch.

"I hope he'll be OK," he said.

What can you say to that? He was a ten-foot-tall bog monster. If *he* wasn't going to be OK, nobody was.

"Can we please go to a hospital now?" wailed Tony Holland. We ignored him and left the AtmoLabbers to follow on foot, or not.

I was caked in mud and had a Baby Season on my back. I was also shaking so hard my brain was rattling in my head. Mum pushed me into the middle and Ed put the heater on full. It didn't help much because both doors had been ripped off. Ash squeezed in between me and Mum, and Owen sat on Mum's lap.

Ed leaned forward against the wheel, keeping his back away from the seat. He looked over at me, his face all drawn and shadowed and old under his beard, gave me a wink, and fired it up. The truck wobbled and roared and rolled, and the road ahead lit up under the beams of the headlights. Ed stamped down on the accelerator, and everything flew around us.

We went past the house and swerved around the broken Weatherbox without slowing, and if Ash and me hadn't grabbed them, Mum and Owen would have been flung out the door.

I sat forward, one hand on the dash, and told Ed to go faster. It was all taking too long, too long. It might be all over by now. What if they had chosen *her*? What if she was the Weatherman now? What could we do? Hand over the Baby Season to her like a present? Let it go? And if it escaped, what then? If the other Seasons discovered what had been done to their child by the new Weatherman they had chosen, what would they do? Would they bother to start all over and pick another? Or would they just . . . rage?

I looked out at the four upside-down mountain-clouds, all standing on their heads, and I thought, *What would happen if they got angry enough to give up on us, on the Weathermen, on the agreement, on the gateways? If they decided to just fall on us in all their rage, how long would we last? You wouldn't even be able to measure it in seconds, and after that there wouldn't be anyone left to measure anything at all. Then it really would be the end of the world.*

"Weathergirl," whispered the girl hag, and the Baby Season moved on my back, hugging me tighter and closer. For the first time I noticed that there was a warmth coming from the Season, spreading through my wet clothes and into my back and all around me, and even though I was racked with the cold, I should have been a lot colder. I shouldn't even have been able to move. I moved my hand, putting it over the Season's hand and giving it a gentle squeeze.

Ed nearly drove us into a ditch taking the turn for the farm. The truck rocked and bounced on the rutted track, and the wild hawthorns and the birches and the brambles of the hedge slapped and scraped at the fender and the windows as we went along.

Suddenly, the cloud mountains vanished and the weird

lights cut out, leaving a clear sky and a full moon that hung over the lake. I was pretty sure there wasn't supposed to be a full moon tonight.

Ed swung into the farmyard, the big headlights shining on the cracked concrete and the weeds and the broken barn.

"Best. Holiday. Ever!" he whispered.

I clambered over Ash and Mum and Owen, ducking low to make sure I didn't bash the Baby Season's head on the roof, jumped out of the truck and ran out of the farmyard and into the field and across to the lake, where the four big giant things were, and the moon. Dad and Neil were on the shore with the other girl hag and the Shieldsmen, looking as if they'd been in the wars. But, most awful and most important, *she* was wading into the middle of the lake.

Too late, too late.

I ran faster.

CHAPTER 31

NEIL

"The moon is for judgment," said Hazel as we watched her sister wade into the lake. "The sun is big and bright and loud and happy and gives all life. The moon is silent and sneaky and subtle. It hides. It peeks. They adore the sun. They dislike the moon, but they respect it."

Sometimes it was like the moon was far away, in the sky beyond the mountains, and sometimes it was like it was right there on top of the field, just over our heads. I was wondering if we should slink away to the woods and hide.

Something roared and clattered and clanked and there was a flare of headlights from the farmyard as Ed's truck came out of the darkness, like a dragon out of a cave, and shuddered to a stop with a grinding of gears. Liz dropped out through the passenger side and came running through the gate, waving her arms in the air and yelling something I couldn't make out. She lowered her head and dropped her arms and sprinted straight for the lake.

"She has the Season!" Hazel said, and with a start I realized that there was something thin and gray on Liz's back.

"Oh my God," I said. "If she can . . ."

But Hugh saw it as well, and started to run to cut Liz off. Mrs. Fitzgerald was halfway out into the lake. Liz had to get the Baby Season out there, now.

"Stop him!" I howled, and leaped after Hugh, and Hazel and the Shieldsmen charged with me.

Liz didn't stop or slow or even swerve. Her eyes were fixed on Mrs. Fitzgerald and the lake. I'd no idea if she even saw Hugh coming right for her. She was small and fierce, but he was big and heavy, and if he caught hold of her that was it.

Hugh reached for Liz, one big hand grazing her shoulder. Hazel and I dived at the same second. She took him in the back of the legs and I wrapped my arms around his waist, and we all went down in a kicking, screaming heap—and then all the Shieldsmen piled on. Through a confusion of legs and arms and heads I saw Liz reach the shore of the lake, and then I thought I saw the Gray Thing on her back wave a long, thin hand, and she was running out onto the water, leaving impossible footprints on the surface that shook like jelly before slowly filling in.

I crawled out from under the struggling bodies and jogged down to the lake.

Liz caught up with Mrs. Fitzgerald just before she reached the middle of the lake. Mrs. Fitzgerald looked at her and let out an irritated noise, then held up her hands and made a shape with them and rose out of the water.

"Liz," she said. "This will not work. Don't do this. They will destroy you."

I put one foot into the water. I had to get out there, even if it meant splashing and spitting and swimming. I had to be there for what happened next.

"Do what?" Liz said. "They lost something, I found it. And now I'm giving it back. They'll be so cross with themselves when they realize they lost their baby, won't they? They'll be mortified. They won't know where to look."

"They'll blame you," Mrs. Fitzgerald said. "They don't care about things like fairness or justice, and they don't recognize good deeds or favors. They'll take it and they'll cast you high and let you fall."

"Liar," Liz said.

I had the right. I was son of the Weatherman. Liz had done her part and brought the Baby Season here, and now the Seasons would decide who would be Weatherman, and if it wasn't Mrs. Fitzgerald, it had to be me.

"What do you think will happen? Will you let Neil be Weatherman while you go back to being you? Without me you'll never know what it's like to have power. To never be scared and never be mocked and do whatever you please. No one else can teach you. No one else will."

Liz looked at her, and then back at me, jerking her head, urging me to hurry on. My little sister. I stood at the edge of the water listening to Mrs. Fitzgerald mock her and taunt her and tell her she'd never be special and never have power and be always scared and small. And in that split second, with barely a thought, I made a choice. It was a choice I didn't even know I had—a choice to change things. There was a new Season now. There was a strange, uncertain future ahead. Maybe it was time for the Weatherman to change, too.

It would have been nice, wouldn't it? To go out there and claim my inheritance. To do magic and know secrets and be treated right by everyone. To be able to protect the people I love and be the living terror of people I hate. It's what I was born to do.

But I took my foot back out of the water and stepped back. Liz's eyes widened, and I made myself grin and wave her on.

That's my sister, you rotten, evil old hag, I thought. *She'll make a better Weatherman than any of us.*

Liz didn't grin back. She looked at me questioningly. *Was*

I sure? I nodded. Of course I wasn't, but I could pretend to be. She blinked, then turned to look at Mrs. Fitzgerald.

"Yeah," I heard her say. "Teach me to stir and sing to an old black pool till I go mad. No thanks."

They stepped forward together and let the Seasons make their choice.

CHAPTER 32

LIZ

The Summer wanted to kill us all.

That's the first thing I felt, this terrible blast of hate and anger from the ball of light. The others were angry, too, and impatient, but even then they were only thinking about what was going on at the lake with a small part of themselves, while the rest was up in the sky, floating in the warm September night. Summer's fury was a thing the size of a planet, all squashed down into one little ball, and now the ball was looking at me. It knocked me back like a punch from a fist as big as an elephant.

While I reeled, Mrs. Fitzgerald spoke calmly, politely, and pleasantly, except it wasn't really speaking.

"Honored Seasons, I present myself as candidate for the role of Weatherman. As you can see, I am strong, power-ful, resourceful, intelligent, and competent. I have a male heir who can ensure the perpetuation of the role down through succeeding generations. I have been observing the disgraced Weatherman you so rightfully rejected, and I strove, in your name, to curb his abuse of power and thwart his ruthless attempt to take the strength of the Seasons for his own. It is thanks to my efforts that he did not succeed. Here beside me is one of his female offspring. Observe how she has bound to herself your own offspring, the child Season that the ousted Weatherman kept imprisoned in this very lake. I have brought them here so you may punish the one and return the other to its rightful place. I do this with no expectation of reward, save the opportunity to devote my life, and the lives of my family, to the operation of the ancient Doorway in your service. I implore you to punish this human child for her grotesque crimes, and release the child Season from its bondage."

As she spoke her poison, the Baby Season on my back squirmed and struggled as if trying to untie itself from a knot, and I realized to my horror that even though I had pulled it from the bog hole, I hadn't pulled her claws from its mind. She still controlled it. The Baby Season was supposed to save us by telling the others the truth about what had happened, but she wouldn't let it.

"Don't listen to her! She's lying! It was all her!" I cried.

"A hysterical creature, isn't she? Here, child Season, let me break your shackles and separate you from this imp."

She lifted the Baby Season off my back with one hand, holding it by the scruff of its neck. It hung limp, twitching feebly.

"Such terrible suffering it has endured," Mrs. Fitzgerald went on. "It will need long healing. I urge you to leave it in my care, where I will see that it receives the peace and quiet and affection it needs."

The Seasons, even the Summer, were taken aback by this. How could a human care for a Season? A Season needed the sky to heal. A Season needed weather to grow. She was a fool to suggest that it was her place, even as Weatherman, to have charge of a Season—even a child!

Mrs. Fitzgerald sensed she'd gone too far. "Forgive my presumption," she said quickly. "Of course, it must be free, and freedom will be its healing."

"You don't like that, do you?" I told her, and turned to the Seasons. "Look at her. She's scared! She knows that once the Baby Season is free she won't be able to control it and it will tell you the truth of what really happened! Right now, she has it in her power! It can't talk or move unless she lets it! Please set it free before you decide. Please listen to what the Baby Season has to say."

We were so tiny, compared to them. They weren't used to looking so closely at things so small. But their attention was narrowing. They were starting to focus. And Mrs. Fitzgerald knew she had to be rid of me before they saw the truth.

"Take her! Punish her for her crimes!" she screeched at Summer. "They violated you! It must not be allowed!"

Whatever mercy they had decided to show Dad was forgotten. The state of the poor Baby Season and Mrs. Fitzgerald's awful lies made Summer roar. I was yanked upward, flung into the sky, straight at the moon. I saw its big round stupid face look back at me, astonished to see a girl fly so high without wings, and I heard lightning crackle and sear as the Summer reached out for me with blinding blue arcs of light.

A mass of thick green vines caught me in a net and pulled me away from the lightning. I was carried down gently to the lake, and found myself looking up into the vegetable face of the Autumn.

"Twiggy Man," I said.

The net of vines tilted and dissolved into twisting tendrils that the Autumn drew back into its body.

Behind Mrs. Fitzgerald, the Baby Season stood up straight and strong and free. Whatever it was saying to the others I couldn't hear, let alone understand. I don't know if it had somehow freed itself, or if the others had finally understood what she was doing just in time to keep me from getting fried like a lump of bacon.

Autumn sent more vines stretching out to the middle of the lake. They wrapped around Mrs. Fitzgerald's middle, binding her arms tight.

"No!" she said. "No, it's a mistake! I wasn't controlling it, I was protecting it from her! She's the one who sank it in a bog! You must listen!"

Autumn lifted her up to throw her to the Summer.

"No!" I cried. "Wait! She is needed!"

I couldn't explain, so I just showed them, focusing my mind on the story Ed had told us about the three sisters and the singing and the stirring. Autumn paused and the Seasons considered their course.

Summer was not happy, but the Seasons did not destroy Mrs. Fitzgerald. Instead, they threw her from the lake and she plummeted toward the field. A huge shape leaped from the grass and caught her in its mouth and bounded away toward the north and the mountains, and the shell and the pool.

A smaller figure ran after it, calling, "Goodbye, Neetch! Goodbye!"

And then all the Seasons looked at me.

And then all the Seasons said: WEATHERMAN.

And then I opened the Door.

The Summer went first. It was as though I inflated like a huge balloon, full of air and water and fire, and I was as strong as the earth and as tall as the sky and as hot as the sun, and I was everywhere and I could see everything, and, when I spoke, it was thunder booming out and shaking the whole planet to its foundations.

And then I was Spring, a growing brightness, a rushing, roaring, spreading energy, cool and sharp, a waking, a shaking, a hunger, bursting and shivering, fingers of rain and waves of warmth and shocks of cold until everything was alive and awake again.

Winter: a roaring, biting, gnawing beast, a shroud, a blanket, a rocky, bony chill. Wide, heavy storms that buried everything and drenched everything and blew the seas into massive, churning troughs and peaks, and battered the rocks and drowned the mountains.

Autumn, like a falling note, the final full bursting of living things, the fruit and the vegetable and the nut and the berry, the busy harvest and the storing as all things shed their seeds and their leaves and die and sleep and the winds begin to rise and the nights to freeze and the days to shorten. Why did Autumn seem like the most gentle Season? The most generous? Anyway, it was the final one to go through, even if it was going through to be here.

The Fifth Season, the Baby Season, didn't go through, or, if it did, it went through without me. I think the Fifth Season comes and goes as it pleases.

At last everything was where it was supposed to be and the world turned once more and the Seasons marched and flowed and the Weathermen performed their tasks.

CHAPTER 33

NEIL

The Seasons went through, one by one, walking up to Liz and vanishing as if going behind an invisible wall, with nothing left behind but a silver shimmer in the air. Autumn was last, going and arriving all at once, and all the birds in the trees and the bushes and the hedges flew up into the air, singing and flapping and fluttering and swooping all over the sky, blocking out the stars but not the moon, because the moon had gone with the Seasons.

So that was it. Mrs. Fitzgerald was on her way back to the mountain she came from. The Baby Season was free. The Doorway had been opened. It was Autumn here and Spring somewhere else and Summer and Winter, all where they were supposed to be. And Liz was the Weatherman. Not me. Not the son and heir, not the one who'd been promised and trained and taught for as long as I could remember, every day knowing that one day it'd be me opening the Doorway. Now knowing that it'd be never.

Mum sometimes says that it's the things you do quickly without really thinking that show what you really want, but I think I would have found it hard if Ed Wharton hadn't shown me that there was more magic in the world than the Weathermen, and it was out there waiting to be discovered.

As they went through, I thought, *Nobody's ever done this before, not since the first Weatherman. And, like Liz says, maybe that was a girl, too!*

And maybe I'd better help Liz, because now that the Seasons had all gone she'd fallen in the water. She was moving her arms slowly, too tired and weak to swim properly, barely able to float. I gave a shout, ran, dived and swam. When I reached her she was sinking, her hair a tangle like pondweed on the surface. I grabbed her collar, lifted her head out of the water, and started pulling for shore.

Mum, Dad, Hazel, twelve Shieldsmen, and three Atmo-Labbers who had hiked on foot around from the bog, all came frothing and churning through the lake as if they were wild horses in an ad for American beer. They raised her up and carried her to land like some sort of reverse viking funeral. Of course they left me to wade wearily out on my ownsome. I collapsed panting on the mucky grass while Liz coughed up lake water and tried to fight off the crowd that closed around to clap her on the back, either to congratulate her or revive her or both.

Then Mum suggested we call an ambulance for Ed.

"And me!" said Tony, who hadn't run to the lake to help my sister. We waited, shivering in our wet clothes, and when the ambulance came it took Ed and Tony and a few of the Shieldsmen who'd been injured and were putting a brave face on it—but Mum told them to cut it out and go have themselves looked after. Ash wanted to go with Ed, but there was no room.

Then we slogged back through the woods to the house, and, as we walked, wet and cold and miserable, it dawned on us that we had won. We had actually won! We began to talk and smile and laugh and swap stories, and point out where the Shieldsmen had fought the elementals.

We got home, a big, happy, babbling crowd, and we had showers and changed clothes—except the Shieldsmen who had no spare clothes and were too big for anything of Mum and Dad's, so they wrapped themselves in our biggest towels while we did load after load in the washing machine—and we all ended up in the kitchen, drinking pot after pot of tea, eating sandwiches and passing around packets of biscuits, talking and laughing nonstop. Everyone cheered Liz as the new Weatherman, and everyone saluted me for making the choice I'd made. They all looked at me with something, I'm not sure, but it might have been respect. Mum and Dad had a different look in their eyes, when they weren't wiping them dry, and I'm not sure, but it might have been pride.

Liz didn't make a big deal of it, of course. Not Liz. You wouldn't expect her to, I mean, she's Liz. But she did make a small deal of it, and a small deal from Liz is worth more than anyone else's big deals any day. She hugged me tight, then thumped me hard.

"Oh, sure," she said. "Autumn was delayed, Summer is mad, the Weatherbox is destroyed, the Club is all gone, there's a whole new Season we don't understand running around and nobody knows what's going to happen next. So *now* you finally give the job to a girl? Typical."

"Oh come on," I said. "With all that going on, would you really want me in charge?"

"Yeah," she said. "I would."

Then she smiled and thumped me again. I couldn't even rub my poor sore shoulder because I was sitting beside Hazel and she was holding my other hand. Liz had given her some clothes, and out of her white dress and in jeans and a T-shirt, she looked much like the rest of us. Like her sisters, she had kind of reset—back to the age she'd been when they'd made her go to the shell to stir and sing, about twelve or thirteen I guessed. Most of that long, horrible life was gone like a bad dream, but there would always be something magic about them. I was hoping they'd both stay.

Under the table, Ash and Owen were commiserating about Neetch and Ed. Mum had rung the hospital and they'd said Ed was going to be fine.

The night went on. There was singing until dawn, and we made a big breakfast and sent everyone to bed.

I think it was the best night of my life.

———•———

It was a long, long time before things settled down.

We moved to the farmhouse, for a start. The Doorway was now under the lake again, so it made sense.

To the surprise of absolutely nobody, we discovered that the Fitzgeralds had been putting a lot more thought and effort into taking over as Weathermen and ruling the world through the Seasons than in keeping their house clean or tidy, which if you ask me did not speak well of how well they would have run things if their crazy plan had worked. Luckily, we had lots of willing bodies to get everything shipshape. The AtmoLabbers and the Shieldsmen all helped with cleaning and fixing the farmhouse and moving us in, and after a couple of months there we were. I like the farmhouse. It's old and shabby and crooked, it's got lots of fireplaces and a big range for cooking and it's cosy and lively and safe.

Dad more or less forced AtmoLab and the Shieldsmen to merge, reforming the Weathermen's Club, with our old house as their headquarters. You should hear the moaning and complaining.

"Middle of nowhere!"

"No broadband!"

"Not working with those technofascists!"

"Not working with that gang of hippies!"

Honestly, I only understand one word in five when they're in full flight, but I think they're all enjoying the arguments almost as much as their new jobs. After hundreds of years in exile, the Shieldsmen are once more the bodyguards of their beloved chieftain, while the AtmoLabbers are exploring realms of science and magic undreamt of in their philosophies and wouldn't give it up for Nobel prizes or free trips in the space shuttle. Tony Holland handing back all the money he'd stolen also helped.

Neetch came back and took up residence in the bog. It's smaller than his home bog, but I think he prefers to live in a small bog with a good friend like Owen next door. Owen is happy, and he and Ash are always running around playing with Neetch and sometimes even riding on his back, which looks terrifying, and Liz goes a bit pale every time she seems them do it.

The people of Moherbeg sleep easier in their beds these nights.

Nobody's seen Hugh or John-Joe or Mrs. Fitzgerald since that night. I think Neetch took her back to the black pool, and I think Hugh and John-Joe followed her, and when I think of them, I see them huddled together in a stone shell, stirring and singing around the deep black pool. People always said John-Joe had a surprisingly sweet singing voice.

We have Ed in one of the bedrooms in the farmhouse. He was much worse than he let on and lost a lot of blood and stayed for ages in the hospital, and then we brought him home to recover. Ash is always in there with him, except when he throws her out to go play with Owen and Neetch.

Hazel has one of the upstairs rooms. I'm helping Mum and Dad to teach her to read and write and stuff. Every now and then we go see a film in town.

And every now and then we hear the wind shake a windowpane or rain rattling on the eaves and Liz puts on her coat and goes down to the lake and stands there, and if you're rude and sneaky enough to keep watching from one of the top windows, you might see a vague shape come and stand beside her, and they walk around a bit together, and then you stop watching because it's none of your business really.

Autumn went and Winter came, though it will be leaving soon, and we'll all go down to the lake together to watch the Weatherman open the Doorway. After that, she says it'll be high time something was done about the whole Doorway situation. She says she needs someone she can trust to make the long, arduous, interesting, and educational journeys to the other three Doorways, to meet the other Weathermen and explain what happened, and to tell them about the new Season and to hear what they have to say. I honestly thought she meant Dad.

"Neil," she said. "Ed's nearly better. When he's ready, why don't the two of you get into that truck and go talk to the Weathermen? You're pretty good at getting into trucks and going off finding people."

"But," I said, "what about Dad?"

"Dad's running the new Weathermen's Club, he's much too busy. He should be enjoying his retirement, and he's never liked travel much. We'll send a few Shieldsmen and an AtmoLabber with you. Maybe we'll hire a mini-bus."

"And me," said Hazel.

"Of course," said Liz. "On the way, you should probably head over to the black pool, see if you're right about the Fitzgeralds, just to be on the safe side."